JOURNEY AHEAD

by

Kileen Prather

Journey Ahead
by Kileen Prather
©2004 by Kileen Prather
Kileenp@gmail.com

Cover Design by Summer R. Morris
Book Layout by Suzanne Austin Wells

Published by
Chauncey Park Press
735 N. Grove Avenue
Oak Park, Illinois 60302

Printed in the United States of America
ISBN: 978-0-98021670-7

Author's Note:

This novel is a work of fiction. All of the main characters are fictitious and any resemblance to real persons is purely coincidental. Though settings, buildings, and businesses exist, liberties may have been taken as to their actual location and description. This story has no purpose other than to entertain the reader.

Chapter One

The sun was just rising as Nikki looked out the left side window of the airport shuttle bus over to Lake Michigan. Even though she was in Milwaukee, Wisconsin where the terrain was flat, the clouds across the lake were positioned against the horizon so they looked like mountains from her vantage point.

Nikki had been a tour manager for the last six years and was constantly traveling from one state to the other all over the country. Last year she had been in forty one states in eight months and sometimes late at night she would wake up and wonder what city she was in, as well as what time zone.

The previous evening she had returned about 10:00 p.m. from a five day Mystery tour to Iowa. It had been an extremely stressful trip. The itinerary had needed a lot of adjusting and some of the meals were not what had been promised.

One dinner was supposed to have a chicken breast as the main entree. However her passengers had been served cold salads since the restaurant assumed that would be preferable in the ninety degree heat! Naturally, the men on tour were extremely disappointed in the meal. Nikki had apologized to her travelers and everyone had gone on and on about the chicken dinner they did not receive.

For the next few days, every time the coach stopped she found a chicken, hen, or rooster in many different forms sitting in her seat. Even though they had laughed a lot on the coach, she was worn out after spending most of the five days keeping the passengers happy and focused away from the trip's flaws.

And now here she was at 6:30 a.m. on her way to Chicago to fly to Seattle for a nine-day tour. Normally she did not do back to back trips, but one of the other tour managers had quit with no notice and they had asked her to do the Iowa trip at the last moment. She was not sure how doing two trips in a row would work out and was a little concerned since she would have the same tour schedule next month.

When she got to the gate at O'Hare she discovered the light flashing for passengers to give up their seat due to overbooking. Her heart sank since she had been hoping for at least a middle seat to be empty next to her so she would have some extra room to stretch out.

There was nothing worse than being "stuffed" in an airplane with little seat space for four plus hours. Her hopes of getting some rest on this flight were rapidly deteriorating since she had never been able to sleep sitting up. She was exhausted from the last few days and staying awake for the next four plus hours was going to be hard to do.

There was a slight delay but then she saw a plane pull up to the gate. It was a large-sized plane and not the size she usually flew on. Since so many Alaskan cruises originated in Seattle and this was July and the heart of the tourist season, there were obviously many more passengers with Seattle as their destination.

As she looked around the gate area she did not see the mobs of people who would be flying with her. Soon, much to her surprise, an announcement came over the loud speaker. Since the smaller plane could not accommodate all the people flying to Seattle, the airline had decided to switch the plane to a 777.

Every seat would have been taken in the other plane. Now there was a half empty plane for her journey to Seattle. There was an hour delay while they waited for the pilot with the proper certification to fly the plane but that was fine with her. There was not anyone or anything special waiting for her in Seattle.

As soon as the plane took off she went to the back and found three empty seats to stretch across. As the movie started she could no longer keep her eyes opened. The next thing she heard was the pilot on the loudspeaker. She was shocked when she heard him say they were beginning their descent into Seattle. She had been napping almost four hours. This was the first time she had ever slept on an airplane. Obviously laying across the three seats had been a lot like lying in a bed. That, combined with the stress from the last tour, had helped her to fall quickly into a deep sleep.

Normally flying to the Pacific Northwest there was always a lot of cloud cover as you neared the coast. Today the sky was a perfect blue with the sun shining brightly. As she looked out the window both Mount St. Helens and Mount Adams were clearly seen in the distance. It was a sight that was always amazing. In a few days she would be riding to this area on her motorcoach, but it was also interesting viewing these mountains from the air since the perspective was different.

As the plane came into Seattle she was treated to another spectacular view. She could see why the people who lived here loved Mount Rainier. It could be days without a view of that mountain but today the majestic snow-capped volcanic peak over fourteen thousand feet tall was breathtaking.

Her tour did not begin until the following day. Tour managers were always expected to be in place the day before the trip started. The tour company did not want some airplane delay that would cause the passengers to get to the hotel before their tour manager arrived. Therefore arriving a day in advance made a lot of sense. And sometimes when she was on a first time tour, arriving early gave a chance to scope out the area for restaurants and other places her travelers would ask about.

Nikki rode the airport shuttle to her hotel. With no responsibilities for the moment she unpacked her suitcase and set out down the street to explore this city she was developing more of a fondness for each time she visited.

Tomorrow her passengers would be arriving and she would have to sit in the lobby most of the day meeting and greeting them with suggestions for free time and meals. But at the moment this time belonged to her.

As she walked down the street she began reflecting on her life. She was fifty-one years old, not very tall, and a little on the heavy side. She wore her blond hair short and had light blue eyes she had inherited from her Swedish grandmother. Many of her passengers could not believe her age; telling her she looked much younger.

She had been married for twenty-eight years. Four years ago her husband, Ted, had had a series of strokes. He had not been paralyzed but had lost his peripheral vision and was no longer able to drive. He also suffered some short-term memory loss which ended his working career. However, she was most bothered by Ted's personality change. He had lost all his joy in living.

The doctor had tried to give him medicine for his depression but he refused to take it. He would constantly tell her that his life was over since he could no longer drive. He would sit on their couch all day with the TV on, reading a newspaper.

Every morning and evening he gave her a peck on the cheek and sometimes a pat on the back. That had been the extent of their emotional and physical life for the last four years.

The only thing Ted seemed to care about was his television, newspaper and walking down the stairs of their condo to the garage to have a cigarette every couple of hours! The doctor had about given up on him and had told her that she had to quit feeling guilty for choices that her husband was making.

The two of them had been growing apart for years. But Ted with his tunnel vision did not get it. All he cared about was his needs being met. In his opinion that was what a "good" wife should do.

Even their sons had told her how selfish and inconsiderate their father was. All he wanted from her now was the housekeeper/ mothering skills she provided. He felt it was her duty to take care of him and she should expect nothing in return.

Food no longer tasted good to him so he never wanted to eat out. And the few times they did go out, he insisted on splitting a meal he wanted since he could not eat much. It became easier for her to just stay home.

On top of that most of the time he complained about her cooking. Thanking her was no longer in his vocabulary and she felt totally unappreciated. When she was home her days were spent washing his clothes, fixing meals and driving him around town to his doctor appointments.

Ted had always liked sports, but since his strokes watching games on television had become an obsession for him. He never talked about anything with her. Most of the time she went days without saying much to him except to tell him what she was fixing for his next meal. She did, however, hear him on the phone every day to their sons discussing the latest sports results.

Most of the time she felt totally invisible to him and was convinced a maid could be doing what she did. She could not even remember the last time he said something nice to her.

Thank goodness she had her jobs and friends to sustain her. She felt trapped in a loveless marriage but because of Ted's physical problems she felt it was her duty to stay with him. She knew she had no decent quality of life. She was living another person's expectations and fantasies but was not sure how to change things. Ted had always been good at manipulating people and making them feel guilty if they did not do what he wanted.

As each year went by however it was becoming harder and harder to live with her husband and she wondered if she was not just playing the role of martyr. Ted had not even bought her a present for her birthday or Christmas for years. He told her, "He could not see to go buy anything."

She felt like telling him he could not see in more ways than one. If he had walked to the Walgreens one block away from their home to buy her something, she could have given him credit for at least trying and showing he cared.

Ted had always taken more from the relationship than he had put in but now he lived in a total state of denial. He only listened to her if it was something he wanted to hear. Otherwise he shut her out. Whenever she tried to talk about how she was feeling he would say, "that's not true," and she realized there was no way to get through to him anymore.

Besides the food she was cooking, the only thing they could talk about was his illness and his medicines. She felt a large void in her life. Four years was a long time to live the life she was living. There was the constant feeling that she had lost the last half of her forties and now her fifties promised to be just as unexciting and empty. With the new medicines Ted was on for cholesterol and blood pressure she felt he would probably live for many, many more years. She did not want anything to happen to him. She just wanted to be appreciated and shown a little love.

Thinking about her job made her so thankful. Not only did she get a break from her husband while she traveled but she met wonderful people from all over the country. She had always had a positive view of life and believed that the next great adventure was just around the corner. And now here she was about to start another one.

As she was walking downtown along 4th Street she decided to do a little shopping before dinner. Whenever she got to Seattle the first place she liked to go was the Seattle Mariners sports shop for her son, Brandon. She liked to check and see what baseball paraphernalia was on sale but most importantly she liked to check out what was new in Bobbleheads. Her son collected Bobbleheads of his favorite players and mascots from teams all over the country and she was always looking to add to his collection.

After purchasing a Bobblehead her son did not have she walked across the street to where the over one hundred foot Western Red Cedar grew in the middle of the boulevard. It amazed her that a tree that tall could be growing right in the heart of such a vibrant downtown.

After gazing up at the tree she strolled into a large department store that was advertising end of summer sales. Acquiring a few bargains she once again began to stroll through the downtown. It was fun being in a new city and having no responsibilities. That would change tomorrow as her passengers begin arriving.

Continuing on her journey she headed down the hill towards Pike Place Market. The waterfront stretched in front of her. There was a small, favorite seafood restaurant that was her destination. She was looking forward to watching as the sun setting behind the Olympic Mountains cast an inviting glimmer over the Emerald City.

As she was eating halibut, a favorite fish from the Pacific Northwest, she thought about her upcoming tour. Tomorrow her next adventure would begin with unknown people who would be entering her life. It was always pleasing the night before a tour thinking about the new people who would soon become friends.

For now she enjoyed her seafood dinner and watching all the different people who made up the crowds milling around the Market area. She could see the ferries as they plied the waters back and forth in the Sound to the many islands around the area returning the commuters home from work.

There were quite a few men rushing around the market with flowers and bottles of wine on their way home. She smiled thinking about the women who these men would make very happy tonight with their thoughtfulness. It had been years since Ted had brought flowers home for her. Actually, except for a couple of Valentine's days, her husband had never brought her flowers.

As the sun set she kept looking up at Mount Rainier. She had a momentary thought that living in this city, even though her family would be so far away, could be a lot of fun. However, she knew her husband would never leave his home now. The familiar was all he desired. Besides he had not done anything to please her for years and she knew he would not start now. No, living in Seattle was a dream. And a dream that had no hope of being fulfilled.

Chapter Two

When Nikki awoke, she realized it was going to be one of those exceptionally warm summer days that Seattle sometimes had. She was staying at a European style boutique hotel in the heart of downtown. It was a cozy place with a polished air but the hotel had one major flaw—no air conditioning. It was rare when they needed it. Even on warm days, the nights would always cool down. However, it could be miserable in that old building when the air condition was not available on those few nights when it was needed.

Usually the hotel scored pretty well on the evaluations at the end of the tour. But it always scored low when the weather was hot. She hated starting the trip off with a bad experience for the passengers, but she knew there was nothing she could do to change the developing situation.

Her travelers began arriving shortly after noon. As she sat at a small desk in the lobby she watched for the arrival of the Super Shuttle vans from the airport. As the suitcases were unloaded from the van, Nikki spied her company's baggage tags and would know instantly that these were her tour members.

As the passengers entered the hotel, she would immediately greet them with a big smile. She could tell they always felt reassured when they saw her as soon as they arrived. The afternoon seemed to speed by as she gave directions for meals and shopping. Before she knew it, 6:00 p.m. had arrived and she was able to call it a day and go to dinner.

She had a good feeling about the passengers she had met. There was a big group from North Carolina, a few from Florida, many from upstate New York, New Jersey, several from the Midwest and even one couple from Phoenix. She liked it when passengers came from all over the country. It was very satisfying at the end of a trip to see how a big group of people from all over the United States would blend and become like a family on these adventures.

On most of her tours, there was a welcome dinner on day one. However since so many East Coast people tended to come on this trip, her company let them eat on their own the first night. People came in at such various times throughout the day and with the different time zones involved, the passengers enjoyed a welcome dinner much more on the second night.

Since the hotel was right downtown, close to so many different dinner choices, her passengers had a chance to choose something that interested them that evening and roam as little or as much as they wanted. After she finished her meet and greet she walked with several of her travelers down to Westlake Mall about three blocks from the hotel.

There was a large food court in the mall with many different meal choices as well as being reasonably priced. It was also a fun way to get to know some of her tour members before the trip started. Several passengers told her at the end of the tour how welcoming that made them feel when she went with them to the mall on that first evening.

The next morning—day two—was a busy day. Since it was Sunday, the motorcoach company always sent a part time driver for the city tour day. It would not be until tomorrow—day three--when she would meet her full time driver for the first time. He would be with them for the rest of the tour and she had called the company to get his name. She realized it was a man she had never had before.

But for now, she concentrated on getting through this day. There were many things going on. First, a city step-on guide would take them around the city. Then there was lunch and shopping at Pike Place Market before some late afternoon free time to clean up and rest before the evening activities. At 5:30 p.m. they were once again on their way with their first stop for dinner at Alki Beach.

The restaurant had large picture windows with a spectacular view across the sound of the Seattle skyline. There was also a white chocolate whipping cream cake to die for that she was looking forward to.

After dinner they continued on to the Space Needle for that adventure. She liked the fact that they went to the Space Needle in the evening. It was always light when they rode the elevator to the top so the three hundred and sixty degree Seattle skyline could be seen. However, night always descended while they were on top and seeing the city lit up in the evening was also breath-taking.

It was a busy, fun day and she was beginning to know her passenger's names, which made the trip more comfortable for everyone. Tomorrow they would head south and her travelers were looking forward to the next part of their journey.

Chapter Three

Day three—7:00 a.m.—time for her to meet her driver and get the luggage loaded for the trip to Mount St. Helens and on to Portland, Oregon. The previous year she had done this tour for the first time. She had a driver, named Joe, who was a little rough around the edges, to say the least but he had been a good driver and had shown her the ropes.

Most of the time the drivers were very good and it was extremely rare for her to not be able to get along with one. And on the very few occasions that happened, the passengers never knew there were problems.

She knew there had been a Seattle driver some of the other Tour Managers had. He had been very difficult to work with. The Tour Managers called him "the crazy driver." Because of that she had emailed Joe from the previous year to see if he could drive for her again. He had emailed back that he already had a job but would see if one of his friends could drive for her. In that way she would not have to worry about dealing with "the crazy driver."

Stepping on to the coach, she introduced herself. She saw a man a little under six feet with short dark blond wavy hair and penetrating brown eyes. He also had a mustache. He was wearing dark dress pants, and a short white dress shirt and tie. She noticed the muscles in his lower arms from all the suitcases he lifted in and out of the luggage bays. He reminded her of an aging surfer, but aging well.

The driver said his name was Chase. She asked him if he was Joe's friend. He looked at her a little strange and just said "No." Then he immediately said to her, "I have to keep the shade on the front window down about six inches to keep the glare out of my eyes."

Nikki had had another driver mention glare once before but Chase was the first one who wanted the shade down. Besides that he said it so defensively she wondered if something was wrong. It was almost as if he was daring her to say "keep it all the way up." Instead she said "fine" and started working on unpacking her tour things and getting organized.

It was another beautiful day. Last year when the tour had arrived at Mount St. Helens there had been a low cloud cover all day encircling the mountain. The passengers never did see the top part of the mountain. Today was picture perfect! Things moved along like clockwork and they made two stops before they finally stopped for lunch at the Coldwater Ridge Visitor Center.

She still was not sure about Chase. He was a good driver and seemed happy when she went down the aisle to collect trash. There were some drivers who took a lot of pride in keeping their coach clean. She always liked those drivers. She was hoping to eat lunch with him since that was usually the best time to sit and get to know each other a little. It was also a good time to discuss the trip without the passengers listening.

Chase did not disappoint her. He asked if she wanted to split a sandwich and she said "yes." They had a nice talk and after lunch he went back to the bus for some downtime before the trip continued.

The rest of the day went smoothly. When they got to Portland she asked him to circle several blocks around the hotel. Both nights in Portland the meals were not included. Nikki had passed menus around the coach and wanted to point out the restaurants to the travelers. Then they would know where the various dining places were located since they would be walking on their own from the hotel.

There was an Italian restaurant that she particularly liked. If you bought a drink during happy hour and sat in the bar section several meals were available at a discounted rate. The food was good and the prices extremely reasonable. Nikki told the passengers not to go there that night because she had not been there for a year and she wanted to stop in and make sure they were still running the specials.

After finishing her chores on the coach she said good night to her driver. Finishing her daily paperwork she then went to dinner at the Mall food court. She saw several of her travelers and was pleased they had found the place with no trouble.

The mall was only two blocks from the hotel but from the outside it looked like a department store. And once you went inside, if you did not know to go all the way through the store and down the stairs, you would have no idea there was a food court in the building. Finally all her duties were done for the evening and it was time for bed.

So far the trip had been going along in typical fashion and everyone on the coach seemed to be having a good time. She had no idea a new chapter in her life was about to start unfolding the next day.

Chapter Four

The next morning as she sat at a table in the hotel restaurant eating breakfast with some of her passengers, Chase came in. He walked right by her without saying good morning and sat at a table by himself with his back to her. She thought perhaps he did not like to be bothered early in the morning. By the time she went out to the bus he seemed his usual friendly self.

Today the passengers would be touring Portland, the Columbia River Gorge area, and Mt. Hood. It was a full day of touring and since there was a local step-on guide for the day, she was able to go to the back of the bus and have some down time.

The tour stopped for lunch at a cute little log cabin cafeteria-style restaurant right on the Columbia River by the Rainbow Bridge. Chase had gone to fuel while she and the step-on guide took the passengers in for lunch. As they were sitting at the table eating, Chase, with his tray of food in hand, walked right by them and sat once again at a table alone with his back to them.

This really bothered her a lot. She had never had a driver eat alone like that before. It was almost as if he had a chip on his shoulder but yet when they were anywhere near the bus he was very friendly and acted like nothing was wrong.

Nikki liked her job and she had the feeling her driver did, too. It could be lonely on the road, though. It was always more fun when the tour manager and driver spent some downtime together. There were always things to talk about—the tour, the passengers or just pass the time away with some friendly conversation usually about different places they had traveled to. It helped the two of them feel more of a team when they spent some mealtime talking and getting to know each other a little bit better.

After lunch she went to the back of the coach again while the local guide continued her tour of the area. They got back to Portland about 5:00 p.m. She told her passengers the Italian Restaurant was running the specials if they wanted to go there. Once again she finished her duties on the bus and just as she was leaving, she turned and said to Chase, "I don't suppose you want to go to dinner with me?"

She was shocked when he said, "let me see the menu." She had never spent much time with her drivers previously but she did not mind eating with them in restaurants when the travelers were also there.

She did not want her drivers to get the wrong idea and it just seemed like a good practice not to go out alone with them. She did not think twice about asking Chase tonight since she knew there would be lots of other passengers at that restaurant besides them. For some reason, he struck her as a lonely person and she was a little intrigued to get to know him a little better.

To her surprise, he said, "yes."

"What time do you want to walk up there?"

"I need to finish my paperwork, sweep the bus, and change my clothes. How about we meet in the lobby in forty-five minutes?"

"That is perfect."

She went to her room and changed into jeans since it was her off duty time. They met in the lobby and walked to the restaurant, which was about two and a half blocks away.

When they arrived, all the tables in the bar area were taken with their travelers so Chase led them to two stools at the far end of the bar. Living in Wisconsin she had always liked trying different beers. This bar had several kinds of beer on tap that were new to her.

After sampling two of the beers, Chase suggested Hefeweizen, a German beer made in Seattle. She enjoyed the taste of it but was surprised that it was served with a lemon. She often had lime with some Mexican beers previously but had never seen lemon in a beer. He explained to her the beer was made from wheat and the lemon brought out the flavor.

Nikki ordered spaghetti and Chase the steamed clams.

"I love steam clams and the minute I saw them on the menu I knew I would come to dinner with you. I have lived in the Seattle area all my life and have traveled up and down the coast for years but I never knew this restaurant had the steam clam special until I saw your menu. And you certainly cannot beat the price. This really made my day."

They started talking about trivial things. He told her he had a lot of seniority at his company and could get most of the trips he wanted. She guessed from his talk that he was probably a couple of years younger than she was.

"If you have so much seniority you can do any tour you want. Why are you on this tour when you could make so much more money on some other trip?"

"Although I can make a lot more in tips on some of the other tours I do, I have already done several Canadian Rockies tours this year and wanted a change of pace. Since our pay is also based on mileage I thought driving to San Francisco would be a nice change of pace. Plus I love the drive down the coast."

He made a few references to Joe, her driver from the previous year, and she could tell from what he said that he did not like him. She could understand how that probably set them off on the wrong foot almost from the start.

"I know Joe is a little rough around the edges but he was very good to me last summer. Last year in a five-month period I was given seven tours that were new tours for me. Plus four of them were brand new trips my company had just set up. Even though I was familiar with all the areas, you know there is always stress when you do a tour for the first time."

Chase nodded agreeing with what she was saying.

"I really appreciate when drivers help me out or teach me new things. There is no way I could know all the nuances of new places like you local drivers do. And traveling all over the United States like I do, I like learning as much as possible. Plus the passengers always feel more secure when a tour manager appears to know what they are doing. I know some guides just make up an answer to some questions, but I would never do that. So the more I learn, the more information I have for my travelers."

Joe, knowing she was on the trip for the first time had showed her the ropes the previous year and had even told her about some shortcuts that resulted in a few itinerary changes. Several other tour managers had done this tour for years and did not know about the things that Joe had taught her on her first time out. She was grateful to him for all his help.

"I requested Joe but he told me he was busy and would get a friend to do my tour. That is why I asked if you were Joe's friend. I could tell by your expression I had said the wrong thing. But I have to tell you, I was worried sick about getting 'the crazy driver' and wanted to do anything I could to avoid that situation."

Chase looked at her and started laughing. He knew "the crazy driver" but she told him some of the stories she had heard from other tour managers in her company who had him.

He had no idea the man was even worse than he had imagined. The worst story was how he had gotten pulled over at the Canadian border going to Vancouver and they had taken everyone's luggage off the coach and searched through it.

The tour manager said she had never been searched at the border before and that had delayed them by an hour and thrown off the timing on her itinerary for the rest of the day. Her friend was sure that the driver had made some crazy remark to Customs, which had resulted in the search.

Chase quickly agreed "the crazy driver" had probably said something since he himself went through customs several times a year and had never been pulled over as she described.

By the time they were finished eating she felt very comfortable with him and was enjoying their conversation. She wanted to ask him about his not eating with her for breakfast and lunch but for some reason she had a feeling she might "spook" him if she asked that question.

She could not believe he was so interesting to talk to and yet could close into himself very quickly at any second. She had never met any other driver who was friendly but at the same time so guarded. Since this was their first trip together she decided to just let things go as they were and see if he became more comfortable with her. Since she had never had a driver she could not get along with she felt it would be a fun challenge to get him to open up and become more comfortable around her.

Chapter Five

Another beautiful day dawned. That was not always a given out here in the summer. Today they would be headed to the Pacific Coast and she was hoping the fog would stay away.

Lunch was at a fun restaurant in Florence, Oregon, right on the coast. After they ate there would be a dune buggy ride in the large sand dunes that were in the area. There was a very strong wind that day and she knew the sand would probably blast their faces.

The thing that made these tours so much fun to her even when you did them many times was not only the different people she met but also the different weather conditions. There were mountain areas that looked beautiful when the sun was shining. But on the cloudy days the colors of the rocks were so much different looking and sometimes more colorful when the sun was not shining on them. She never got tired of looking and experiencing the different sights while on the road.

Chase took it for granted that they would have lunch together that day. After the passengers were seated in an area out by the water, the two of them found a table on the other side of the restaurant. She was able to look out the window and watch the seals playing in the water as they ate.

Once again the conversation was very easy going. Even though they did not know each other very well, they had things in common and the conversation never seemed to slow.

She could not believe how much she enjoyed talking to him when he let his guard down. They seemed to have so many things to talk about and he was constantly making side comments to her remarks.

She had a feeling she could sit and talk with him forever, and she could not help but laugh at many of the things he said to her. Suddenly she realized she had not laughed like that in years. She decided she liked making a new friend in him. Since this was a lunch and shopping time, when they finished eating Chase returned to the bus for his downtime while she browsed the little shops in town.

As she walked around she thought about him. He seemed to be a completely different person than the one she had met two days previously. She had no idea what had made him change but she liked this new person he was becoming. She had no thoughts romantically about him but enjoyed his company tremendously.

Oh, boy! Was she right about the wind. Although the dune buggy ride was fun, there were times it felt that the sandblasting on their bodies just cut right through them. It was even necessary at times to keep your eyes closed to keep the sand out when the ride faced the ocean. But that was all part of the adventure.

Each time she did the dune buggy ride it was always a different experience. And the women passengers all laughed when she told them how some ladies spent a lot of money to have their faces sandblasted in that way at some expensive spa and they were able to get the same benefits while enjoying a thrilling ride.

After that attraction there was an hour drive to the

hotel. Most of the passengers slept since they were worn out from the dune buggy ride. When they arrived in Coos Bay they were able to check into the night's lodging and have some free time to freshen up before going to dinner and the casino that was in the town.

She took her passengers into dinner at a wonderful Italian restaurant owned by the town's mayor. The Italian specialties were good but she never grew tired of eating the salmon when she was on the Pacific Coast. Once again that was her choice that evening and she was definitely not disappointed.

Drivers always have to keep their logbook up to date after each stop. Usually when going into a restaurant the driver would show up five to ten minutes after everyone was seated as they caught up on their log before coming in. She kept waiting for Chase to come in to eat but he never showed up.

After dinner he was waiting by the bus, with his usual friendly smile, to help the passengers on.

"Where were you? Why didn't you come into dinner? This was our first included dinner since you started the tour and I would think you would want to take advantage of that."

"I wanted to guard the bus since I had to park on this busy street, which is also the main highway through town."

She just shook her head. After the easygoing time they had together at lunch she could not believe he had not come in to dinner. She had never met a driver who could be so easy to talk to and then close into himself so quickly. As John Gray would say he was constantly "retreating into his cave."

Nikki liked Chase and thought he was an exceptionally good driver. She loved how good he was with the passengers. There was a lady, named Joan, who had irritated her, the first couple of days. Normally she enjoyed her passengers immensely but this lady had a little bit of a whiny voice and she had been so worn out from her previous Mystery tour that she had let the woman bother her.

When she said something to Chase about Joan, he told her right away that he thought the woman was "a sweetheart." He pointed out what a lonely lady she was and since she was older probably did not have a lot of years left to travel. Nikki noticed there was a slight tremor in Joan's hands and once she started paying more attention to her, the woman became the bus mascot.

They might have missed the fun experience the bus "family" had with Joan if it had not been for Chase pointing out how wrong she was about the woman. Her respect for him was greatly enhanced by that experience and that was why it bothered her when he seemed to retreat into himself so often. She felt he was a very lonely man who had the ability to have a lot of fun if he would let himself out of his shell.

Realizing she could not worry about the way he was acting she let the issue go. The most important thing to her on tour was having a good working relationship with her driver. They needed to be a team and give the passengers the best possible trip. The tour company sold the "dream trip" to the travelers and it was up to Nikki to make sure the dream became a reality. The passengers were number one as far as she was concerned.

She liked Chase but did not know if he would ever be her driver again. Since they had a good rapport between them that was all she expected. Deciding there was nothing more she could do to change the way he was acting she just let any other thoughts go. She knew they would have a good tour and since she and the passengers were having a good time together that was all she wanted or needed.

Chapter Six

The rest of the trip was pretty uneventful but fun. There was a group of eight passengers from New Jersey who liked sitting in the back of the bus. Even though seat rotation was company policy, when the motorcoach was not completely filled, and travelers requested to have the back seats for the entire trip, she would usually say yes to that request.

Several times a day she would walk up and down the aisle of the coach to see how everyone was faring. When the "back of the bus" people found out that she was doing a Christmas tour to San Antonio the following December and since they had always wanted to do that trip, they asked if she would call her company and sign them up.

Nikki also had two ladies from North Carolina who had her call the office and sign them up for the National Parks tour she was doing in September. She really enjoyed starting a trip and discovering a few people on the tour she had traveled with before.

Chase actually came into eat that evening. Dinner was in an old logging camp in Eureka, California, and was always a lively place. The next morning after they left Eureka, the day would be spent winding through the redwood groves on their way to "the city by the Bay."

Before they left town, they would always stop at

the Carson Mansion for "a Kodak moment" and show the passengers the wonderful downtown of Eureka. However this excursion always delayed their arrival into San Francisco.

She was really pleased when Chase suggested doing the sightseeing around Eureka after dinner. She knew he was anxious to get in his room for the evening. However, touring after dinner tonight would give them more time to get into San Francisco a little earlier the next day and hopefully avoid some traffic.

The next day went very smoothly. The passengers loved the redwoods and the afternoon rest stop at the Pacific Ocean to stick their feet in the water. Nikki planned to eat lunch in the town she had stopped at the year before. However, Chase asked her if they could continue to a town a little closer to San Francisco. There was a Truck Plaza in the town he preferred where he could get fuel at a pretty reasonable price.

She was always agreeable to a driver's suggestion for a stop as long as there were good places for the people to have lunch. And besides, as long as it did not throw off her schedule, she wanted to help the drivers when they had a special request. She felt it was the least she could do when they were always so helpful to her.

Chase dropped them in a section of town that had three restaurants right together where the passengers could spread out. About forty-five minutes later he was back to pick them up but did not get anything to eat. She assumed he had probably had lunch at the truck travel plaza.

As they neared San Francisco traffic was much lighter since they had gained those extra few minutes not having to tour in Eureka that morning. As they neared the Golden Gate Bridge she got excited. She always liked coming into San Francisco.

The fog was not surrounding the area and the travelers had a wonderful view of the bridge and the city. This, of course, was not always a given. One of the ladies said she was sure she saw "Tony Bennett" sitting on top of the bridge singing and welcoming them into the city. This made her smile and she saw the smile on Chase's face, too.

It was mid afternoon on a Friday when they arrived at the hotel. Since the passengers were on their own that evening she had explained where they were in the wharf area and Chase had driven a few blocks around from the hotel so she could point out restaurants and other sights that would be of interest.

He mentioned having a beer together that night. The passengers would all be busy doing what interested them so there would be some free time for the two of them. She told him to call her if he wanted to get together.

By now she was not worried about going out with him if the passengers were not around. They had a good working relationship and she knew that it would not get personal between them. Even though she had never done anything like that before, she somehow felt it would be fun and safe going with him. She felt very comfortable around him now.

She also had a lot of work to finish. Besides her paperwork, she needed a couple of hours to arrange all the airport transfers for the passengers not riding on the bus with her on Sunday. As far as she was concerned, she did not care whether he called or not. She knew eventually she had to go out and get something to eat and if he did call she would grab a bite with him.

By the time all her work was completed it was 7:30 p.m. and she was extremely tired. Chase had not phoned and she figured it was just as well. She walked down to the wharf and grabbed a seafood salad and some soup and brought it back to her room. Knowing she was all organized for the rest of the trip was a good feeling and she went to bed knowing she could just enjoy the next day.

The next morning was the cable car ride and city tour. The city tour guide was an exceptionally good guide however the tour did not turn out too well. A couple of the places they used to tour were closed for remodeling. But it was the fog that really ruined much of the tour. It was hard for the travelers to imagine what they were supposed to be seeing when the fog completely encircled the sights. Naturally the city tour specialist ended up taking a hit on his score when the weather did not cooperate.

The tour ended in Sausalito. This city was right over the Golden Gate Bridge and for some reason the fog that encircled San Francisco never affected that town. When they arrived downtown the sun was shining and the temperature was in the seventies.

The guide had Chase drive the downtown area as he pointed out all the different restaurants. He talked about their different specialties before dropping the travelers in the center of town. Nikki went with Chase and the guide to the bus parking area.

Since they would stay in Sausalito for two hours the guide left to take the ferry back to the city. Chase had his usual logbook to catch up on and she asked if it was okay if she stayed on the coach for a few minutes finishing up her paperwork since she was not interested in spending the extra time shopping.

After sitting in the back of the bus while the guide did his city tour Nikki had a few things she needed to organize. This would be the last time the group would be together in a setting where she could talk to them and she wanted to go through airline schedules and the evaluations with her passengers on the way back to San Francisco. Since the two of them finished what they were doing about the same time, Chase suggested they walk to lunch together.

After lunch and returning to San Francisco, he dropped them off back down at the Wharf for their boat ride on the bay. He would leave them there for the rest of the afternoon and pick them up after dinner. Even though it was the "good-bye dinner," he was not able to join them since there was no place to park the coach in the wharf area.

Before she knew it the day was over and Chase was back at the temporary bus-parking stop to pick them up and take them back to their lodging for the night. As they drove up to the hotel she told the passengers to be sure and take everything off the bus since only some of them would be going with her to the airport in the morning.

She also gathered up all her tour things to take into the hotel to organize and repack for her flight the next day. As she was getting off the coach Chase stopped her and asked if she wanted to go for a beer.

All her paperwork was done. Except for seeing the passengers off in the morning, her work on this trip was finished. Sitting in a hotel room watching TV the rest of the evening did not do much for her.

She was used to sitting alone in her room or sitting alone in her home since she and Ted very rarely went out and he never talked to her anymore. Since she was on the road so much it was hard for her to form very lasting friendships at home and the loneliness was something she had just learned to accept.

However, as much as she enjoyed her travels, when she got to the end of one her tours there was a feeling of being "done" and since she was at that point right now, going for a beer sounded like a much better idea. Besides she felt very comfortable around him now. When they were together they always maintained a very professional relationship while never talking about anything too personal.

They met in the lobby about a half hour later and walked around the corner to a sports bar. Chase called it "hiding out" when you found a place where you knew the travelers would not find you. This bar also had Hefeweizen beer, and although she was still having trouble pronouncing the word, she enjoyed the taste with the lemon in it.

"Nikki, we need to talk about the airport drop tomorrow. My company does not have the proper airport stickers for the bus. They do not drop passengers in San Francisco often enough to justify the cost. Although normally I would have to pay any tickets I get, in this case, my company will pay if I do get one. They just think it is cheaper paying for a ticket versus buying an airport sticker. But, I would really like to avoid a ticket if at all possible."

The two of them worked out a plan to drop everyone promptly at the different airlines so he could leave the airport quickly and hopefully avoid getting a ticket. The evening passed all too soon and she realized she had not had such an enjoyable evening out like that in a long time.

Chase had a girlfriend, who he talked about from time to time, and she, of course, was married. But they still enjoyed each other's company. Actually it was probably a lot more fun because there was not any pressure like you might find in a date situation.

She told him she was coming back the following month and asked if he would be her driver again.

"It is so much better to have a driver you have had before because he knows where you like to make stops and other things you like to do to make the tour special. If you cannot do it could you see if one of your friend's could? I just do not want to get "the crazy driver' if I can help it. After the stories I have heard, I am a little paranoid about that."

"I will try and do the tour but if I can't, I will definitely ask one of my friends. I know you like Joe but he is tied up the rest of the summer with another tour company so he is not an option."

Sunday dawned and she was busy all morning seeing the passengers off who were going by airport shuttle vans. There was an included breakfast at the hotel that was good for either of the two mornings they were there.

Last year she and Joe had eaten breakfast together before leaving for the airport. Chase had never mentioned eating breakfast with her and she decided she would let him bring the subject up. She liked having the breakfast on the last day since she had such a long flight home with no food.

Chase never said anything about breakfast and she never saw him in the restaurant that morning. It was a situation she was getting use to. One day they were like best friends and the next day she had no idea where he was. Pretty soon it was 11:00 a.m. and time to load the luggage and the rest of the passengers for the ride to the airport.

She couldn't help feeling a little sad not knowing if Chase would ever be her driver again. She felt she had found a friend and hoped they could spend more time with each other next month. Only time would tell.

Everything went smoothly at the airport. They made two drops before the big one. Getting the last of the passengers off the bus at the last stop she directed them into the group check in while Chase unloaded the luggage. She then found a skycap to get the luggage inside. Everything was done very quickly. As soon as Chase knew she had the skycap coming he jumped back on the bus to leave.

Waving good-bye to him all of a sudden he jumped back off the bus, ran to her, and gave her a quick kiss on the cheek. Then he was gone! As he drove away she continued waving at him. Just then the airport security came up to her asking where the bus had gone. She realized he had just missed getting a ticket by seconds.

Chapter Seven

The flight was very smooth and when they landed she walked her passenger's down to her company's waiting personnel by baggage who would see them to their van transportation for their rides home. Her company had door-to-door pick up for the travelers who lived in the Chicago area, and she breathed a sigh of relief when all her passengers were taken care of. She retrieved her suitcases and went to the bus lobby for her return trip to Wisconsin.

Back to her life with Ted... Some days she did not think she could go on much more living with him. When they did have a conversation it was always about his ailments or how he was feeling. He had lost a lot of weight since his desire for food was pretty much gone. No matter what she made, he found something to criticize about the meal, which was getting very tiring to her. Appreciation and kindness seemed to be a thing of the past as far as he was concerned.

She had always had some dream she would be thinking about. For years she and her boys had envisioned having a summer cottage and it had actually happened. There had been so many fun years there with her two sons and their family and friends. She had many wonderful memories of those times when her children were growing up and she knew she would cherish those years forever.

Now she had a new wish and when her brother came to visit the previous month she had told him about it. She knew this one would probably never happen but she was always willing to share her vision with anyone willing to listen. She hoped that some day she could have a boat, cabin cruiser size, and then she would spend her winters on the boat going from one Caribbean island to the other whenever and wherever the mood struck.

As she was telling her brother, Randy, about her dream, Ted spoke up. "Nikki, you can't have a boat. We need all our money to pay my medical expenses."

Her jaw dropped. She could not believe he could stand there being negative about something that was just a dream, with no hope of it ever coming to pass. Hearing him putting her idea down, her brother turned to her and said, "If I can ever help make it happen, I will."

Ted's negativism was definitely getting to her. She could feel herself getting angry all the time. Although she internalized her anger and tried to have patience, she was finding it harder and harder to be around him. As far as she was concerned, he treated her worse than a housekeeper.

At least a maid got paid. She could not remember the last time he had thanked her for doing something nice for him. She found herself "running away" by going on tours just to get away from him for short periods of time. She knew conditions were going to have to change or things would come to a head. Sadly she realized his view would be that it was her problem not his.

She was extremely busy the next few weeks preparing for her upcoming tours. She had seven trips from August through October. This was always the busiest time of the year and she knew since there would only be a few days between trips, this was the perfect time to get everything organized.

Besides her back to back August tours, she would also have back to back trips in September for National Parks and Colorado by Trains and she would be gone twenty two days at that time. After that she would be home one week before heading back to Colorado.

Her health had been on her mind a lot lately. She felt winded just climbing the stairs in her condo and found she was sitting a lot during the day when she should have been up moving around. It was hard for her to get motivated to exercise and she worried some of her husband's depressed state was rubbing off on her. Just before her August tours began, she had her birthday.

Being fifty-one had seemed okay and had not really bothered her. She knew aging was inevitable and figured there was no point in trying to fight it. But for some reason turning fifty-two made her feel that she had really gone over the hill. She felt old and fat. Normally she would not have such negative thoughts but probably her relationship with her husband and his negative thinking was affecting her. She tried to put these thoughts out of her mind as she prepared for the next round of trips.

Before she knew it the time for the Iowa Mystery trip was upon her. This time the tour was much better. The office had restructured a lot of the itinerary. Not only did she score well but also the trip score ended up in the ninety's. The only down side was the driver.

She had a wonderful driver she had been with previously. However after the first day he came to her and said he was not feeling well. He had a perfect driving record and did not want anything to happen while he was driving to ruin his good safety record or hurt his travelers. He called his company and they replaced him. Luckily they were not far away so that afternoon his company sent a driver in a company car and then her original driver drove the car back home the next morning.

Her new driver was only used in replacement situations. She understood why. He drove the bus in a very jerky manner and sometimes crossed over into the left lane for a brief moment. She was extremely nervous with him, as were some of her travelers who noticed his erratic driving. At one point a passenger asked her to sit on the step on the floor by the driver and talk to him because they thought he was nodding off. She was really happy when the trip was finally over and she and the travelers arrived home safely.

Once again she did not get back to Milwaukee until after 10:00 p.m. and it was 6:30 a.m. the next morning when she was back riding the airport shuttle bus for her trip to O'Hare and on to Seattle. Luckily she had laid out her clothes and tour materials before leaving on the Iowa tour. All she did was put her dirty clothes in the hamper, pack the clean clothes, and dump her unneeded tour things in a corner and repack the new items.

As the bus traveled down the interstate towards Chicago she could not help but wonder if Chase would be her driver again.

Chapter Eight

This time she was not tired on her plane ride to Seattle. Naturally it was a typical flight to the Northwest-- plenty of cloud cover, so nothing to see. After gathering her luggage at baggage she caught the Super Shuttle downtown.

Arriving in the city she checked into her hotel. Unlike the July trip, the weatherman was calling for the upcoming days to be cooler. There would be no problems with the hotel not having air conditioning on this tour which would be one less thing she had to worry about.

After unpacking, she again walked to her favorite seafood restaurant. Tonight, since she was once again on back-to-back trips and had not slept on the plane, she was extremely tired due to the time change. She went to bed at 8:00 p.m., which was really 10:00 p.m. according to her body. She was surprised she had stayed awake as long as she had.

The next day she had an airport run. Whenever a group of over ten came she was required to go to the airport and pick them up. For this tour she had a group of thirty-five from Indianapolis, Indiana she had to meet.

The Seattle airport was a difficult airport to pick up passengers with the new regulations after 9/11. Once you got the travelers and their baggage you had to walk almost a half a mile to where the bus was allowed to park. She arranged for a skycap to take the luggage to the bus. Meanwhile she got one of those small airport luggage carts so the passengers could put their carry-ons on the cart since they had such a long walk to the coach.

As she rounded the corner to the bus parking she saw Chase standing by the door of the bus. He had already loaded the luggage and was just waiting for her and the travelers. She could see him looking for her. She waved at him as she pushed the cart loaded with carry-ons towards the bus and watched as he waved back with a smile.

As the passengers climbed on the bus she said to him, "I didn't know if you would be here or not."

"I told you I would do the tour."

She remembered he really had not been specific about doing the trip. He had only said he would try. However she let his comment slide. She still was not quite sure what might make him retreat into himself.

Instead she replied, "I did not know if you would do the airport run today since it is a Saturday."

"I know you were not real happy with some things on the coach on our last tour so I brought this one to see if you thought it would be okay. If it meets your approval, I'll bring it on Monday."

"Thank you, Chase. I appreciate your thoughtfulness."

After she had made her welcoming remarks to her travelers on the way into the city, she walked through the motorcoach. She was really touched by his thoughtfulness wanting to please her. It seemed like a long time since someone wanted to satisfy her like that. After returning to her front seat behind the driver, with a smile she said, "The bus looks great Chase. And thanks for bringing a bus with a cordless mike."

He nodded to her and she saw the pleased smile on

his face as she looked into his mirror.

He dropped them at the hotel. His last words to her were, "I will see you Monday morning about 7:00 a.m.—as soon as I get my latte." That made her smile. She knew he could not function properly in the morning without his latte. Sometimes he would be extremely quiet if he did not have it. She understood his behavior because she felt the same way about her black coffee.

The next day she had a driver who never stopped talking.

"I have been working for the coach company for many years but I am going through a pretty painful divorce and am not doing tours out of town at the present. I am surprised that you are doing a second trip with Chase though. There are not many tour managers who will go on trips with him. They think he is too fussy and has too many quirks."

She wondered about that. She had a couple of drivers in Illinois that she used a lot who were a little obsessive about keeping their coaches clean. Actually she preferred that. She was neat and orderly and she liked the fact that drivers took pride in their job. She also felt the same way about her work. She knew Chase was an excellent driver and took his work seriously. And she would rather have a driver like him anytime.

The other thing she noticed was the real pleasure Chase took in knowing the travelers. There were some tour managers who looked down on their drivers. Unless there was an emergency relating to the bus, the tour managers were always in charge. There were a few of them who did not have a lot of confidence in themselves. They were the ones who would tell the drivers to just drive and not to interact with the passengers. They basically did not want a driver to look like he knew more than they did.

There was nothing worse for a driver than being told, "You are just a dumb driver and that is all I want you to do." She had many drivers tell her horror stories of their treatment by this type of guide. However the drivers also told her they had little ways to get back at those tour managers without the travelers knowing.

She had always thought of herself as part of a team. Both the escort and driver received tips from the travelers. She felt the more they worked well together and gave the best possible trip to the passengers, the better their tips would be.

She was beginning to have some insight into Chase's actions. If he had been driving for almost twenty years and had tour managers treating him like a "dumb bus driver," she could understand why he chose to eat alone. Actually he had given her one of his business cards and it showed he had been certified as a "driver guide." She was sure he probably knew a lot more than some of the tour directors he had worked with over the years.

Nikki had learned a lot from her drivers all over the country. They sat in the front driving the bus and did the same trip many, many times each year. Not only did they know their areas but they would also listen to all the different tour managers giving the travelers information. Some managers would be strong in history and others with science or other areas. All that information could not help but rub off.

She knew most drivers did know more than many of their tour managers. Often when passengers would ask her specific questions about an area that she could not answer, she would say, "Let me ask my resident expert." After the driver answered the question for her, she would let the travelers know what his answer had been while giving him credit for the answer.

Believing she was a good tour manager, she also knew there was no way she could know the answer to every question in all the different areas of the country she went to. She always relied on her drivers to help her and had never been disappointed.

On their first day together on the previous tour, Chase had told her at lunch that she had mentioned some fact he had not known. She had been pleased when he said that. She figured it was his way of telling her she had done her research. Living in that area and driving for years while listening to so many different tour managers, she found it unusual there would be a fact he did not know.

Their day of touring Seattle was drawing to a close and this group of passengers seemed even more fun than the last group. As she said good-bye to her city driver, she began looking forward to her journey south the next day.

Although she enjoyed all her passengers, once in awhile she would have a group that gelled right from the start and it would turn into an extra special fun tour. She sensed that this group of travelers would be like that on this tour and she was looking forward to the adventure that awaited all of them.

Chapter Nine

It was exactly 7:00 a.m. when Chase drove the bus up to the front door of the hotel. She had counted and marked the bags so all he would have to do was load them in the luggage bays. Before doing the luggage, he took her tour suitcase and put it on the backseat in the rear of the bus so she could unpack her supplies.

It was not long before the tour members were seated and they were headed for Mount St. Helens. It was another beautiful day. She had read that Seattle was having one of its best summers on record. As they left the city, the travelers had a wonderful view of Mount Rainier to the left of the coach. To the right, the Olympic Mountains could be seen off in the distance.

As soon as all the preliminary busy work was done and the information given to the passengers completed, she got on her cell phone to reconfirm with some of the suppliers she had not caught up with. The last call was to Chris, the local step-on guide in San Francisco.

When she hung up Chase mentioned that he thought there was going to be a big festival in San Francisco the following weekend. He asked her if she would call the guide back to find out if the festival would be going on.

Telling him she would be happy to call Chris back she asked, "Answer me this. Why do you want to know?"

She knew him well enough now to know he worried about some situations. She used to be that way, too. However, she had learned that if it were a situation she could control, she would worry about it. If she had no control over the situation, she let it go. It had been a hard lesson to learn but it really helped keep her stress down while traveling.

"Chase, is there anything you are going to be able to do different or will you be able to drive differently if you know the festival is going on?"

"No."

"Then the reason you want to know is so you can worry and obsess over a situation that will be happening six days from now of which you have no control over?"

He did not answer her.

"Why don't you just enjoy the next few days and worry about the festival when we get closer to San Francisco?" He still did not say a word. "But, I will call Chris up right now and ask him if you really need to know."

"No, that's okay. I'll wait till we get there."

As they neared Coldwater Ridge Visitor Center, she asked him if he wanted to split a sandwich again. "No. My girlfriend packed me a lunch."

Here we go again, she thought. I guess it would never occur to him to bring his lunch into the Visitor Center. There were picnic tables outside the cafeteria and she had planned to eat outside since the day was exceptionally warm and the view of Mount St. Helens spectacular from that vantage point.

Even though he did not eat with her, they kept up a steady stream of bantering all day. At one point, one of the passengers told her that she and Chase reminded him of the old radio show, "The Bickersons." He meant it in a positive way and she took it as a compliment. When she told him what the passenger had said, he just smiled.

When they first entered the park, all the travelers were given wristbands so the park officials knew they had paid to get into the different visitor centers. Before they left the last stop, she always took her scissors down the aisle telling her passengers she was going to "operate" on them. The bands could not be ripped so it was easier just to cut them off.

For some reason, today he followed behind her down the aisle taking the wristbands from her as she cut them off. She was clueless why he was doing that. She almost said something to him about being capable of cutting off the wristbands and not throwing them on the floor but she decided to let it go.

As they were leaving Mount St. Helens, she began telling the passengers about their dinner choices in Portland for the next two nights. As she was passing out the menus towards the back of the bus, she overheard Chase telling some passengers up front how good the steam clams were at the Italian restaurant and that was where he & Nikki were going.

Once again, she shook her head. He had not said anything about going to dinner with her and she had learned never to assume anything with him. There were times when he was so hard to read.

Finishing up her duties on the coach after they arrived in Portland, she asked him when he wanted to go to dinner.

"I would like to go as soon as possible after I change because I have paperwork tonight to finish."

However he vacillated about exactly what time she should meet him in the lobby.

In San Francisco she had waited in the lobby for him when they were going for a beer and had gotten tied up with passengers who wanted to chat. She did not want that to happen again. She needed to call her local city guide for the following day. Knowing his room was a few doors down from hers she asked him to just knock when he was ready.

He showed up at her door about a half hour later. He had his usual after work clothes on. He was wearing jeans with a white undershirt and carrying his blue jean long sleeve shirt. She could not help admire how good he looked in his casual clothes.

When they got to the restaurant the tables in the bar area were once again filled with their travelers. There were two sisters, rather crude and obnoxious, whom he had named "the War Department." They were sitting at a table being extremely loud. It was obvious they had already had at least one drink.

As he led her to the same barstools as the last time, the ladies started coming on to him. She felt him stiffen and knew it would be hard for him to be nice to them as the tour progressed.

Since he had not shared a sandwich with her for lunch, she had eaten a big lunch and was not very hungry. They ordered their Hefeweizen beers and Chase his steamed clams. She decided on the Caesar salad. As usual it seemed like they had a lot of things to talk about but "the War Department" ladies kept coming up and putting their arms on him. Due to the ladies' behavior, as soon as they finished eating they left.

She told him how much she was looking forward to the next day. She was doing her tour of the National Parks in a couple of weeks and having a free day, she would "immerse herself in National Parks of the Southwest research" while the local guide took care of their travelers.

As they were walking back to the hotel, after leaving the restaurant, he turned and looked at her. Out of the blue he said, "You know, you're okay."

She was not sure what to say in response. She knew coming from him, and as closed mouth as he was, that statement was high praise. As they continued walking she simply said, "Thanks."

Chapter Ten

The next morning she was sitting at a table for six, eating the breakfast buffet in the hotel restaurant provided, with four of her passengers. To her complete surprise, he sat down next to her with a plate of food in hand. She told him good morning and remembering the last tour decided she would just give up trying to figure him out.

The tour went well as she sat in the back of the bus studying her research on the National Parks. Before she knew it, lunchtime had arrived. Once again Chase went to fuel as she and the local guide took the passengers into the cafeteria line.

As she and the guide reached the start of the food, he came up and stood behind the two of them. She knew that meant he was going to sit and eat lunch with them. She could not believe how much he had changed from one tour to the next, but pretended his actions were completely normal. He had not said anything about dinner that evening and she decided it was best to just let him play out the evening the way he wanted.

After returning to Portland from the day of touring, she started off the bus when he asked what time they were going to dinner. Acting like the question was perfectly normal she asked, "Did you want to go back to the Italian restaurant?"

"Yes. The steamed clams are not quite as good as the place I go to in Seattle, but they are pretty good and a third of the cost. If I could afford them, I would eat steamed clams two or three times a week."

She told him all she needed to do was change her clothes. She had finished all her paperwork while the local guide was in charge. She asked him if he would just knock on her door when he was ready. Looking at her, he nodded.

It was not very long before she heard his knock. When she opened the door he was standing there with a smile. Then she heard him say to her, "Your date has arrived!"

She was totally taken aback. Acting as if everything was perfectly normal nonetheless his comment had shocked her. She knew he was kidding about the date remark, but with her situation with her husband and the way she had felt about herself since her birthday, she really never envisioned anyone thinking of her in that way again.

She knew his casual remark would change her perception of herself. There had been several instances in the past few years when she had repeat travelers on one of her coaches. Sometimes one of them would come up to her and say, "You know you said something to me on our last tour together which changed my outlook on life." She now knew exactly what they meant.

As they walked to the restaurant several thoughts went through her head. Fifteen years ago she had quit smoking and had piled on the weight. She had tried one diet after the other and had taken off a few pounds here and there but always put it right back on.

She decided right then and there that if she was going to be heavy the rest of her life, she would at least be healthy. She was going to start eating better but most important she was going to start walking and exercising more.

She hated the way she looked, but more important, the way she felt. If Chase could enjoy being with her and talking to her looking the way she looked, maybe there was still more fun for her to encounter. She realized that Ted's retreat from the world had rubbed off on her. She was still too young to have stopped having any fun with her life.

This time she and Chase were by themselves in the restaurant. It was nice having a break from the passengers. As much as they both enjoyed their travelers, sometimes it was pleasurable being alone to talk without having someone come up needing your attention.

Having had another big lunch she was not very hungry. After they ordered their beer she told him she was just going to have the Caesar salad. However she really would like to try one of his clams.

"I do not know if I will like clams but I do enjoy trying new foods. Since you have been ordering double orders every time we come, do you mind if I try one of your clams?"

"Actually, I am excited for you to try one."

When the order came he explained how they came in a garlic sauce with chopped up tomatoes. He had her try one of the tomatoes right away. He said what he liked was still being able to taste the garlic, tomatoes and clams in his mouth two hours later.

She knew exactly what he meant. She felt the same way about the Greek gyros sandwiches. The sauce on those sandwiches was a cucumber garlic sauce and when it was really good, even when brushing your teeth, you could still taste it the next day. She told him maybe someday they could have a gyros sandwich together.

When she tried the clams she decided she had just found a new food she liked. He was delighted. He told her if she came and did another tour to Seattle the next summer, he would take her to his favorite restaurant for clams. She told him she did not know if she would get back to Seattle or not, since she never knew where she would be sent. However if she did, she would hold him to that promise.

He mentioned that he was having troubles with his girlfriend. He said, "It just isn't fun anymore." She knew exactly what he meant. She told him it needed to be fun.

She did not say anything to him about her personal life, but she thought about what he had said. Getting to the ages they were, it was not as if they had their whole lives stretched in front of them anymore. If it couldn't be fun, was it worth staying in a relationship when you felt so lonely.

"You know I am beginning to think that being alone might not be such a bad way to live. It would be better than living with someone while feeling so lonely."

"I totally agree with you."

She decided to lighten up the conversation. She told him about a game she was going to play on the bus the next day during a boring stretch of road before getting to the Coast. It was a good way for the passengers to bond and get to know each other. She would pass out sheets asking for some personal information and then two questions. What was your most interesting trip experience? And, what would you do if you won a million dollars?

Asking her what she would do if she won the money she immediately told him about her wish to have a boat. He thought boating around the Caribbean in the winter sounded like fun. A cruise ship line owned his company and he had done a lot of cruising over the years for a greatly reduced price.

Then she mentioned that she would take the boat

to Wisconsin in the summer. He asked her how she would get there and she said through the St. Lawrence Seaway and down into the Great Lakes. He nodded as if that made a lot of sense. She could not believe he was playing along with her.

"Maybe I will come and visit you here in Seattle on my boat, too. Although it will probably take me quite awhile to get here, I could come and stay a couple of weeks. Then when you had a day off I could take you for a ride and you could take me for steamed clams."

"I would love to have you come out and visit me on your boat. And I would definitely treat for the steamed clams."

Even though the idea was totally far-fetched and out of reach it was fun talking about it. Now besides her brother, she felt she had someone else who was not laughing at her dream.

As they began discussing touring again he said, "I had an interesting trip experience once. I had a lady passenger drop her camera down the toilet in the bus. She asked me to try and dig the camera out of the holding tank for her."

She could not stop laughing at that story. Even if he could have retrieved the camera, imagine the shape it would have been.

Sitting and talking to him about trivial things was really enjoyable. He always seemed to have funny comments to things she said. At one point she asked him as she covered her mouth, "Why do you always make me laugh when we are eating?"

He just smiled at her.

As they left the restaurant without looking at him, she said, "You know I have never gone out with my driver like this before." She did not know why she told him that.

She guessed she wanted him to know she valued their conversations.

They walked back to the hotel without saying anything else, but it felt comfortable. Just as they got to the hotel while looking straight ahead he said, "I have never gone out with my tour manager either." That statement certainly did not surprise her.

Chapter Eleven

Nikki asked her travelers if they would mind leaving fifteen minutes earlier that day. She usually took them by a lighthouse in California but she heard about one that was supposed to be interesting in Oregon that she wanted to visit.

Since this was the afternoon of the dune buggy ride, it was a busy day, and she felt that leaving a little early would help fit everything in since she was not sure how the timing would go. She did not tell the passengers what she wanted to do because if it did not work out they might be upset. She just told them she was planning a surprise.

After the morning rest stop she started playing her game. As she finished up the last passenger someone asked her what her answers would be. Naturally, she told them about her boat. Then they wanted Chase's answers.

She knew how he would respond to most of the questions since she was getting to know him a little better from their talks. When she got to the most interesting trip experience, she told everyone about the camera in the toilet.

To her surprise, one of the other traveler's came forward and told a very similar story that had happened in an outhouse in Canada. By this time everyone was laughing and talking to each other back and forth which was the whole purpose of the game.

It was not long before they pulled up to the restaurant on the Pacific Coast. Today there were lots of seals playing out in the water. The travelers went in to eat lunch. Although they never said anything to each other she finished up her paperwork as she waited for Chase to complete his log. Then they walked to the restaurant together. Once again their former table was empty so they headed to it.

They were still a little concerned where the lighthouse was that she wanted to go to but he told her he thought he could find it. She ordered a tuna fish sandwich and cup of chowder. Today the wind was not blowing like the previous month but it was much cooler and she was glad she had brought a heavier jacket and hat and mittens.

They sat across from each other and she found herself leaning against the table towards him as she was talking. She had finished her chowder and half the sandwich. She picked up the other half of the sandwich but continued talking to him. All of a sudden almost angrily he said, "When are you going to eat that sandwich?"

"What difference does it make? I have an hour and a half to kill here," she said to him with a puzzled expression.

For some reason he sounded almost irritated with her and she did not know why. Trying to figure out what was happening she heard him say more calmly this time, "I have the same hour and a half."

"Then I guess we are spending some of it together," she answered as she shrugged her shoulders.

She did not have a clue what had set him off but decided it was not worth wondering about. Maybe he just wants to get back to the coach. She knew that sometimes she never seemed at a loss for words and wondered if he was tired of listening to her.

Looking at him she said, "If you want to go back

to the bus, feel free. I don't mind sitting here alone. I often eat alone." She had no idea what had started this conversation but she was ready for it to be over.

To her surprise, he never said a word but just sat there. There was an awkward moment between them but then he started talking about a passenger and she felt him relax again. It was another twenty minutes before they left the restaurant.

He went back to the bus and she started wandering through the shops in town to kill some time. She did not know what had happened back at the restaurant but she sensed a subtle change in their relationship. It was almost as if it bothered him to be with her, but at the same time he could not stay away.

As she wandered into one shop she realized she was in a bookstore/gift shop. She found a book on Oregon lighthouses and looked up the one she was interested in. Not only was there a description of the lighthouse, there was also a history as well as directions. They knew the name of the town but had not known the exact location. Now she knew exactly where it was and she also wrote down some pertinent facts she had not known.

As they neared the town where the lighthouse was located she leaned closer to Chase. The passengers still did not know where they were going.

"I know where it is," she whispered to him.

"And, when were you going to tell me?"

"I figured it was on a need to know basis, and you definitely need to know now. It is six miles past this town and about a quarter of a mile towards the ocean. I found some interesting information about the lighthouse in a bookstore at lunch. By the way, are you clocking the miles since we just left town?"

"Of course."

She just smiled.

"You and your lighthouses," he said loud enough for some passengers to hear him.

"Quiet." But, by then he was making the turn so she figured she better tell the travelers about the sight they were going to see.

The passengers were excited to be going there and were glad they had started fifteen minutes earlier that morning. Not only was it a nice looking lighthouse, with some interesting history, but there were also oyster beds and a kelp bed that they were able to view from their vantage point.

They ended up pulling into their hotel about twenty minutes earlier that evening. Because of the early departure she had been able to move the dune buggy ride up a half hour. Everyone enjoyed getting to the hotel early. It had been cold and the passengers were looking forward to having a chance to get in the pool or taking a shower before leaving for dinner.

This hotel was not one of her favorites and tonight was no exception. Some of the room assignments were messed up. The staff had used an old rooming list and had missed a couple of passengers. The hotel was almost sold out. By the time she got done changing and adding passengers' rooms she discovered she had gotten stuck in a smoking room.

Chase had unloaded the luggage and was cleaning the coach. He could not go to his room until she finished getting her things off the coach, so he had taken off his dress shirt and was sweeping the bus in his undershirt. Although she had never really thought about him in a sexual way she knew something had changed in their relationship that afternoon.

The room problems had really upset her and being

stuck in a smoking room had not helped the situation. She had finished changing her window nametags and was making one final walk through the bus to check the seats for personal items passengers might have left. As she came walking from the rear she was half talking to herself as he came towards her.

All of a sudden it struck her how good he looked in an undershirt! She could not believe she was thinking about him in that way, especially since she had never thought anything like that before about him or anyone else in all her married years.

She decided she was losing it. Maybe these back-to-back tours were starting to get to her. The closer she walked towards him the more her stomach became upset. Glancing at him for a moment she quickly turned her body to get by him. Then she walked to her seat to retrieve her things and got off the coach as fast as possible.

By the time they boarded for dinner she was back to her old self. Chase, acting like nothing had happened, began chatting in his usual way. He told her how much he enjoyed getting in early since he had been able to get the coach cleaned and still had time to take a shower before all the evening activities. He had been preparing the bus at 5:00 a.m. that morning and would be out until after 9:00 p.m. since this was the casino night. He had really appreciated having some down time to relax.

This was the evening that he had not come into dinner on the last tour. As she got off the coach she asked if he was coming in to eat.

"It depends how I feel about the parking situation."

She just shook her head as she walked the passengers into the restaurant and up to the second floor where the banquet facilities were located. About ten minutes later, he entered the room and sat down in the empty seat next to her. She smiled to herself. There was no way she would ever figure this man out but it sure made the trip more interesting.

Chapter Twelve

It was 3:00 a.m. when she awoke. She had a terrible headache and her sinuses were hurting. She knew the smoking room was not helping the situation. She also was bothered by her new feelings towards Chase.

She had been on the road for six years and had never been attracted to anyone. She knew she had a terrible marriage but she certainly was not interested in making her life any more of a mess. She ended up tossing and turning the rest of the night.

She finally went to breakfast at 6:30 a.m. She liked to get into the restaurants early when breakfast entailed anything more than the deluxe continental breakfasts some hotel chains provided. You never knew when problems would develop. This morning was going to prove her theory true. As she walked into the restaurant, some passengers came and told her breakfast was not ready.

The chef had not shown up for the first time in sixteen years. The waitresses were very upset. They had finally found someone to come in and cook. Instead of ordering off the menu, the chef was working on preparing a buffet. It was the only way they could feed all the travelers in such a short time.

Nikki did not feel like eating much. She took a bowl of fruit and was working on her fourth cup of coffee while reading the morning paper when Chase sat down beside her. She told him what had happened and by the time he had finished eating, the situation had calmed down. She went to her room to collect her things.

This morning they were stopping at a myrtle wood factory for about an hour before leaving town. Myrtle wood could only be found in that small area on the Pacific coast and by Myrtle Beach, South Carolina, on the Atlantic Ocean.

As she boarded the bus, Chase told her one of the women passengers had come and asked him if he could come back and pick up her husband at the hotel just before the factory shopping tour was over. Her husband was not feeling well and she wanted him to rest as long as possible. He asked Nikki if she would ride along with him.

She had her share of problems on the road. There were some tours when hospital runs and accident reports were a given. She was very lucky, though, because she had never had a passenger die on one of her trips. Her first thought, which she voiced to Chase, was "he'll lay down for a nap and not wake up."

"Don't look at the worst possible scenario. I am sure he will be fine. He just needed a little extra rest and was not interested in shopping for myrtle wood."

Her next thought was the way her day had already started with the breakfast problems and the fact she had just taken her second set of Advil since her sinuses were still killing her, what would happen next. She told Chase she would definitely go with him.

As soon as she got the passengers settled in for the factory tour, including leaving her cell phone number with the owners in case an emergency came up, she reboarded the coach. Chase had said he needed fuel and they had a good forty minutes before they needed to pick up the passenger.

Usually tour managers sit behind the driver. That is considered the most unsafe seat on the coach and the driver blocks the view. The seat across the aisle is probably the best seat on the coach. It has a completely unobstructed view and there is a ledge.

Whenever she was alone on the coach with a driver, she would sit in that seat. She liked it because she could put her feet up over the ledge and stretch out. Plus she would be able to look at the driver, rather than the back of his head, while she talked to him.

After telling him she had not slept well and had a killer headache, she sat down and stretched her legs out across the ledge. He immediately asked her why she had not slept well. She was not about to tell him why she was tossing and turning and just told him she did not know why but was on her fourth Advil and knew it would kick in soon.

As he fueled, she closed her eyes and tried to relax. When he returned to the coach she kept her eyes closed as he went to a "hideout" a block away from the hotel. He had not wanted to pull up to the hotel until the last possible moment because he knew the minute he arrived, the traveler would come out of his room. He wanted the man to have as much time as possible to relax.

Her headache was beginning to recede but for some reason being alone with Chase in such a small place was affecting her. She was thinking, "So near and yet so far…"

Every time she looked at him her stomach ached. This made her more upset. She felt she was acting like a silly schoolgirl with a crush on some boy in her classroom. She definitely had mixed feelings. It was kind of fun feeling excited about someone, especially when not a word was said between them about the developing situation. At the same time, she chided herself for even thinking that way.

Knowing she would never involve herself in a "one night stand," she knew she was in no position to begin a relationship. Besides, even if a liaison was possible, how could that happen when you lived two thousand miles apart?

She might be wrong since neither was saying anything to the other, but she had a feeling he was having similar feelings towards her. The unsaid emotions were definitely creating a charged atmosphere around them.

The way he looked at her was creating a hazy perspective. She was thinking of something she had recently read, "Love strikes those whose paths are destined to cross." It was definitely time to get back to reality!

After they had picked up their passengers, they headed for the morning rest stop. She loved this stop. It was a favorite on the tour. It had a perfect view of the Pacific Ocean with the monolithic rocks scattered in the water and a view of the coastline for miles in both directions.

A few years previously, a beer company had made a commercial with the Clydesdales galloping down this section of the coast because of its beauty. It would be the first time the travelers got this panoramic vista since arriving at the Pacific. After the stop they would continue along the ocean for an hour and a half with the unbelievable views until lunch.

She should have realized, with the way her day had been going, things would not go as planned. As soon as they reached the stop the fog completely encircled them. The water could not even be seen and they were right in front of it. She hated it when the travelers missed one of the sights she considered so special. On top of that, as they were ready to pull out, she was missing a passenger! His wife was concerned because he was beginning to have health problems, including wandering off.

There were several small buildings in the area and Chase suggested she check them. She checked all of the buildings and headed back to the coach. She asked Chase if he thought she should try walking down to the water. He told her to give it a few minutes. They were now ten minutes late leaving and all the passengers were getting worried.

About five minutes later, the door to one of the buildings she had checked opened. Coming out of the door was the missing passenger! She went to get him. The building had been a restaurant. He told her he had gone in there to use the restroom. Obviously that was where he had been when she had looked in that building. You could hear a collective sigh of relief from the passengers as she and the missing traveler reboarded the coach.

The only good that came from the missing passenger was since they had lost fifteen minutes, the fog was now beginning to lift. About halfway to lunch the fog totally lifted and the passengers were able to view the incredible sights. She and Chase kept looking for a good vantage point. Just before the lunch stop he pulled over. He had found a perfect spot for their "Kodak moment."

There were not many places along the coast to stop for lunch that could serve fifty people in an hour. Today's route was no exception. They stopped at a restaurant connected to a hotel that usually did a good job. By the time Nikki got all the passengers seated there was only one table left for her and Chase. Naturally it was right in the middle and their travelers would surround them.

She told the waitress she would wait for her driver. She was more concerned that her travelers all ordered. Sometimes passengers would get upset when meals took a long time and she liked to be last so no one was waiting for a particular tour member. The travelers never said anything if she was the last person eating, causing the schedule to run behind.

Chase finally finished his log and came in. She ordered her usual tuna fish sandwich. He ordered chowder and a toasted cheese sandwich. For some reason, the conversation was not flowing between them as usual. There was definitely a tension between them.

The waitress brought his soup and she stared out the window as he ate. She was almost afraid to look at him. It seemed lately that whenever he looked at her with his piercing eyes, her stomach felt like she had been punched. Something was definitely happening to her and she felt it was best to try and ignore the developing situation.

Their sandwiches finally arrived and she began eating. She almost had to choke down her first half. She decided she could not even attempt the second half. She hated wasting food but there was no way to take it with her.

She looked at Chase and told him she was not very hungry. He had taken a few bites of his sandwich. He looked at her and said his sandwich did not taste very good either.

Although they still said nothing to each other, she could not believe he was not also feeling something towards her after his reaction to his food. Since their meal was being "comped," he put his tip down and left for the coach.

She went and sat with some passengers who had just received their food. Since it had taken a long time for this particular table to get their food she waited with them while they ate. After using the bathroom, they all left the restaurant together.

Since they were the last to leave lunch and the restaurant had taken longer than usual to serve them they were ten minutes later than the time she had told the travelers they would depart. Naturally none of the other passengers complained when all of them, including her, got on the coach late.

The afternoon turned out much better than the morning had. It was as if when the fog lifted so did all the negative vibes. The travelers liked quiet time after lunch and she was able to look out the window and not have to think. They stopped for their afternoon rest stop at the state park right by the ocean. She loved this stop. Many of her passengers enjoyed taking their shoes off and walking to the water to put their feet into the cold Pacific.

Chase never seemed to mind this stop. Some drivers would complain when you brought passengers back to the coach with sandy feet but he said he always swept the bus anyway and it was not a big deal.

By the time they arrived at the rest stop, the two of them had been discussing the rest of their plans for the day. Their conversation was back to their normal bantering and she was beginning to wonder if perhaps the feelings she thought he was also experiencing were in her imagination.

She just wanted it to be fun between them again and she decided to act as casual and friendly as usual. Whatever the reason, the tension eased and things got back to normal again.

That evening Chase asked her to save him a place at dinner, which was once again at the logging camp. Their dinner was held in a private room with long tables. Sometimes she had trouble hearing when there was background noise. He had commented on this from time to time. She told him on their last trip that when the tour season was over she planned to see a hearing specialist to see if she had a problem.

By the time all the passengers were settled, she went to sit and discovered all the seats had been taken at the long tables except some chairs near "the War Department" ladies. She knew he would not be happy. The night before they had sat at the same table with these women and they had been really loud and embarrassing. She realized the other travelers steered as far away from them as possible. Naturally the only chairs left were by these ladies.

When he arrived, he sat across from her rather than next to her. The women were sitting two seats down from him and Nikki figured he sat on that side so he would not have to look at them. They were being their usual loud boorish selves.

Not saying a word he looked at her. She knew what he was thinking but figured he had to realize it was the only place that had been available to sit at since she had entered the room last. That table had the only empty seats left in the room probably because the other passengers did not want to sit next to these ladies.

As he gave her a funny look all she said was, "forget the ear doctor. I need to see an eye doctor." He smiled at her and she smiled back. It was fun to be able to secretly communicate when the passengers were right there.

She knew he was anxious to do the Eureka city tour and get back to the hotel. However, there was an old piano in the corner of the room and one of the women jumped up after dinner and started playing. Before Nikki knew it, there was a spontaneous sing along and dinner was extended by half an hour.

It was moments like this that made her job so wonderful. The enjoyable sing along made everyone feel good. She loved it when the passengers interacted so well with each other. Many of the passengers were still singing as they toured Eureka.

Chapter Thirteen

The next morning she was once again down to breakfast early. Sitting at a table for two, she faced the window and watched Chase load the luggage. The waitress came up and commented that she was the only tour manager who would be down early to make sure things were going alright. She just smiled. She had learned small upsets did not become big upsets if she oversaw potential problem situations.

When he finished the luggage, with a plate of food in hand, he came and sat beside her. The next two mornings in San Francisco there was only the one included breakfast. She would once again eat it on her last day so she had a decent meal before the long airline flight.

The year before her driver had eaten with her on that last morning. Naturally on the previous trip Chase had not. She knew she was going to miss their morning breakfast time together. She asked him if he wanted to eat breakfast with her on Sunday. He told her he would see. She figured that meant his usual no.

They had discovered some shortcuts, which had not detracted from the tour. Winding through the redwood groves, they discovered they were running about half an hour ahead of schedule. They stopped at their usual lunch stop. This was a small town with two fast food places and an extremely slow sit down restaurant.

This town was the only fast food lunch place she stopped at on the tour. She knew the passengers enjoyed a nice dinner on San Francisco's wharf that evening and many times wanted a smaller lunch.

This was the city Chase asked to stop at on their previous trip so he could fuel since it was less expensive than San Francisco. The last time however he had picked them up when lunchtime was over.

Today as he left he told her to save him a seat. Since most of the travelers went to the fast food place, the lines were quite long. By the time she sat down with her food he was back.

After ordering his food, he came walking over to her table. Instead of sitting across from her as he usually did at lunch he sat down close beside her. She did not say a word but turned her head and looked at him instead.

Noticing her look he said, "I do not want my back to the door." She just nodded and let it go but she was a little uncomfortable with him sitting so close to her.

After lunch he went and opened the door to the coach, but once again came back over to the outside tables where she was talking to some passengers and just stood next to her.

Usually he would stand by the door of the bus and this was very unusual behavior. It reminded her of when he had followed her down the aisle of the coach cutting off wristbands from Mount St. Helens. She wished she knew what he was thinking but knew he would never tell her. And she realized it was probably better that way.

The trip into San Francisco was unbelievable. They zipped through some of the towns where there were usually bad traffic tie-ups. She could feel the tension leave his body as he got through the last big town along the way. She leaned forward and said; "now you can relax until Sausalito and the city." He nodded at her.

They entered the city about forty-five minutes early and traffic was almost non-existent. She had never seen the trip go so smoothly. It was amazing what being ahead of schedule could do when you entered a big city on a Friday night.

Once again he mentioned having a beer at the sports bar around the corner. She did not have many calls to make on this trip since most of the passengers would be going to the airport with them on Sunday. She did however have to go down to the Wharf and pick up the boat tickets for the bay cruise the next day.

On her way back to the hotel, she ran into him. He had been looking for a place to park the coach. Once he had the bus parked securely for the evening, he could relax. She had never met a driver who did not complain about how bus unfriendly San Francisco was.

He asked her if she was ready to go for a beer. She told him she needed a few minutes to change her clothes. Once again his room was down the hall from her room. She told him to knock when he was ready. He gave her a funny look but said he would.

It was only about 5:00 p.m. when they entered their "hideout." All the stools at the bar were taken so they sat at one of those tall little tables that bars often have. He ordered Hefeweizen for both of them.

The bartender brought their beer very quickly and left. As she glanced down at her beer he had already gotten off his chair and was headed for the bar. He was back in a minute with two lemons. He squeezed a lemon into her glass and did the same for his.

Once again she was shocked by something he did or said. She knew this was a simple gesture and he probably did not know what it meant to her. In her life everyone expected she would get everything for them. If she had been home, Ted would have said, "Nikki, get me lemon." It really felt good to have someone do something for her for a change and she did not even have to ask him. She realized it was this small type of consideration that had been missing from her life for a long time.

It was not too long before some stools at the bar were free. They moved to the bar immediately. The tension between them had eased and the talk flowed between them again. He was watching the Seattle Mariners on TV and the time passed very quickly.

She hoped he would say something about going out the next night. She enjoyed being with him and since it would be their last night together she wanted to spend more time with him. However she wanted him to be comfortable around her and be her friend, so she knew she would have to wait and see what he wanted to happen.

Chapter Fourteen

She awakened very early the next morning. There was a great little café around the corner she had told her passengers about. Breakfast in the wharf area was hard to find under ten dollars. This place had excellent food and many of the breakfast choices were under five dollars. Since only one breakfast was included during their stay, this place was a good bargain.

She ordered her coffee and a croissant. Sitting with some passengers, she had just finished her croissant when some of them noticed Chase walking across the street. A few of them shouted and waved at him. He waved back. She smiled.

She knew exactly where he was going. Not only was he checking on the coach but also the last trip he could not find a latte and so now he was on his search.

Actually on her way back from the wharf with her boat tickets the previous afternoon she had spotted a latte shop. When they were at the sports bar last night she told him it was just one block behind the café she was now sitting in. One of the passengers also mentioned they had just seen him eating breakfast in the hotel. She knew that meant they would not be having breakfast tomorrow on their last day together.

It was only a few minutes later when Chase appeared

at the door of the café and looking at her said, "I can't find the latte shop."

Shaking her head at him, she said, "Do you know where this place is? Well, that place is one block behind us," as she pointed her thumb in the direction of the store.

He immediately snapped at her, "I don't know this or that… I can't find it!"

She smiled as she excused herself from the passengers and paid the waiter. They left in search of the latte shop. As they turned the corner she did not see it either.

"I told you it is not there. You must have mixed up your streets."

"I know exactly where my streets are," she said half irritated by his comment. She insisted they keep walking in the direction of the supposed latte shop.

They passed some girls on the street and Chase stopped to talk to them. They were carrying coffee cups from his beloved Starbucks. They pointed back in the direction they had just come from.

One more store down the latte shop was tucked back from the street. As soon as she said, "there it is," with an "I told you so" note in her voice, he answered "but it's Asian."

"What difference does that make?"

"Asians use a different kind of machine and it does not taste as good."

As she sighed, he pointed out the Starbucks one block further the girls had just showed him.

Since she was dashing all over the place with him, she decided she would continue on his journey. She had been making an effort to walk as much as possible and figured walking a couple more blocks would be more exercise for her before going back to the hotel.

As soon as they entered the Starbucks, he got in line as she spotted Chris, their local step-on guide sitting and having a cup of coffee. She immediately went over and sat with him. When she explained what was happening Chris looked at her and said, "He's right. Asians use a different machine and the lattes do not taste as good." Shaking her head, she knew she had just lost that battle.

Chase went back to get the coach as she and the guide walked back to the hotel. She told Chris his tour had not scored very well the last time. She knew he was a terrific guide and it was not his fault. Cliff House was now closed for renovation, which eliminated that stop, but the worst problem had been the fog. Any stop with overlooks of the city had been useless to even consider stopping at. Today the fog was not too bad, but she wondered if he could add to the tour a little.

He told her he did a special city tour with drive-bys of Danielle Steel, Robin Williams, and Don Johnson's homes. He said normally he had to have special drivers on those tours because many drivers could not take the sharp turns and hills.

Chris knew her driver was capable of driving anywhere he needed him to uphill or down in this city. She was so glad they had found Chase his latte. He would be in a good mood and she knew this could turn into a very special tour.

As Chase followed the guide's directions, many times the passengers clapped at his ability to get the coach in and out of some very tight situations. She had been on coaches for six years watching drivers take the bus into places she thought were impossible, but even she was impressed by some of his twists and turns. Between Chris and Chase, it turned into one of the best city tours she had ever been on.

Once again the tour ended at Sausalito for lunch. Chris took the ferry back to the city. Chase had some paperwork and since they would be there for two hours neither of them wanted to eat while the passengers were still sitting in the restaurants.

She decided to call her husband and see how things were going. It seemed like Ted had one problem after the other to discuss with her. She was standing outside the coach talking on her cell. When she finished she got back on the bus to get her purse for lunch.

"That was obviously your husband."

"How did you know?"

"Because you have spent the last five minutes pacing back and forth while you were talking. Since I have never seen you pace and appear so agitated while on the phone before, I figured it must be someone you knew."

Upset that he had seen her riled she looked at him and said, "Are you ready to eat?"

He closed up his log book and together they walked over to a little seafood place. There were only a couple of passengers left in the restaurant and they were getting ready to leave.

He had said nothing about going out that evening. As she ate she kept thinking she would like to say something to him. She did not want to get sappy but she wanted him to know he had helped her feel better about herself as a person.

Not knowing if she would get sent back to Seattle the next year, she just did not know what to say to him. This probably would be the last time they would be alone together.

Finally she said, "If I do not get out and see you next year, I just want you to know I am glad our paths crossed." She did not know if that sounded stupid or not, but at least she had said something.

Nikki had been raised to never show emotion. She tended to keep everything inside. Actually, it seemed better that way. If you let someone in, you became vulnerable and could get hurt.

After they finished eating, they walked back to the bus. There was still more than a half hour before leaving and she was not interested in shopping. On the way back she mentioned she would like to go on a cruise for Christmas or New Years but would not take a cruise unless either her son or brother also came along.

Naturally he wondered why one of them needed to go along. She told him how her husband would just sit in his stateroom watching TV or follow her around and it would be very boring.

"Why don't you just go in one of the bars on board some evening without your husband?"

His idea shocked her. "Someone might think I wanted to be picked up."

Looking at her, he laughed. "Nikki, I have been on lots of cruises. People do not think that way anymore unless you let them know that is what you want. Most of the time they go in just to talk to other people and have a good time."

"Really?" She thought about what he had just said, but she still remained doubtful.

After they got back to the coach he sat in his seat doing some paperwork. She sat in her favorite front seat on the door side where she could put the seat back and stretch her legs out. In a few minutes he got up and went to a seat about three rows behind her. He put his seat back and closed his eyes.

They never said another word. The door of the coach was opened and about fifteen minutes later passengers started getting on so they got up and went to their seats.

He dropped them at the wharf for the boat ride and picked them up after dinner. When they got back to the hotel she gathered up her tour things to pack. He never said a thing about going out so she got off the coach and went to her room.

Even though she would have liked to spend their last night together, she figured it was probably better this way. They both had lives and responsibilities to return to. Obviously he was more comfortable "retreating to his cave."

Chapter Fifteen

Once again she awoke very early. She decided since it was Sunday she would go to 7:30 a.m. Church. She had not been able to go on her previous tours because she was always seeing passengers off. Today no one was leaving until after 9:00 a.m.

The other good thing was the Church was seven blocks away—straight up hill. She really wanted to get healthy again and was making an effort to walk every day. Knowing she had a long plane ride later she was looking forward to her walk.

Nikki saw several of her passengers at Church. She returned to the hotel in time to say good-bye to her travelers going to the airport on the Super Shuttle. She then called Chase about 9:30 a.m. to discuss luggage. He was still in bed and seemed half irritated she called. She told him she would wait until she saw him at the coach.

She did not go to breakfast until 10:00 a.m. She was not very hungry, but not only was it an included meal; she knew there would not be any food on the long plane ride home. She took her book along to read while she ate. All of a sudden she looked at her watch. It was five minutes to eleven. She should have been out there ten minutes ago.

The passengers would all be on the bus. She knew Chase would probably be upset since she had not been there to help organize the luggage. She also knew he wanted to drop them at the airport as soon as possible so he could begin his two-day journey back to Seattle.

She was right! He had a scowl on his face. All she said was, "Sorry. I was reading and lost track of time." He looked at her in that funny way of his but she avoided his eyes.

She helped him sort the luggage by their stops at the different airlines so they could move along quickly once they started dropping off the travelers. He asked her to explain to the passengers how the stops would be handled so he could avoid getting a ticket for his company. He knew the travelers would be rushed off the coach and he wanted them to know why it was happening.

As they traveled out to the airport he was abnormally quiet. She started talking to the passengers sitting across from her. They had also been at Church that morning and they told her how much they enjoyed seeing new churches.

Obviously listening to the conversation he asked her if she had gone to Church. Without thinking what she was saying, she said, "Yes, and I even said a prayer that you would have a safe return home."

Hearing her remark, the passengers across from her told him they also had said the same prayer for him. He asked her what time this was all going on and she told him the church service had started at 7:30 a.m.

She could tell he was touched by the fact she and the passengers had said a prayer for him and he did not quite know what to say. This was very unusual for him. One of the first things she had liked about him was how he always had a quick snappy comeback to everything she said.

Today she liked that he seemed speechless. She was glad she had told him about the prayer. It seemed like his mood improved by what had been said. She did not want to leave him when she felt he was half irritated with her, even though she had no clue why he seemed to be in such a bad mood.

She stood down by the inside door of the bus as they reached the airport. They had two short drops before the big one. As soon as she spotted the airline drop she and Chase jumped out. She helped the passengers off the bus as he pulled the luggage from under the bay. She gave her travelers a hug and both she and Chase said good-bye to them as they jumped quickly back on the bus.

When they got to the last drop, she instructed the passengers to go into the airport to the Group desk, which was right inside the door. She would get a skycap and get their luggage into them as quickly as possible, so they could begin the check-in process.

As soon as Chase stopped the bus she jumped out and went in search of a skycap. When she got back, the passengers were already in the airport and Chase had just finished unloading the last of the luggage.

She assumed he would quickly get back on the coach and take off, as previously, since it had taken longer at the airport this time due to all the extra passengers and luggage. Instead he just stood there facing her.

Finally he asked her if she had gotten a skycap. As she turned around she saw the skycap coming. Turning back towards Chase she said, "Yes, here he comes now."

As she looked at him, he still stood quietly in front of her. Her only thought was since he was still standing in front of her she would give him a quick hug good-bye. Tour managers constantly hug their passengers and also give hello and good-bye hugs to their favorite drivers.

She reached up and put her arms around Chase. As she entwined her arms around his neck she hugged him tightly. She had no idea why she was squeezing him like that. She could not break the embrace and felt like she was standing outside her body watching and feeling someone else hug him like that.

At first he just stood there, but as she continued to cling to him tightly, she felt him put an arm around her waist and kiss her on the cheek. All of a sudden she had the weird sensation that somehow "they fit."

Although only seconds went by she felt like it had been many minutes. She wished she could have told him how he had affected her life but as she broke the embrace all she could do was look at him and say, "thank you for the nice trips."

He looked at her tenderly. Then he turned and walked back to the bus. He went up the stairs and sat down in his seat as she started to wave good-bye to him. Suddenly he stood up from his seat, turned around and looked at her one last time before sitting back down and driving away.

The quiet came to an end and as if coming out of a trance she once again heard the planes overhead. The noise assaulted her senses. For those few brief moments, it had been just the two of them. She had read before of two people sharing a moment when the world around them ceased to exist but it was an experience she had never had. As her surroundings came back into focus she turned and saw the skycap loading the last of her luggage.

It seemed like she was always waving good-bye to him. Only time would tell if she would ever see him again. However, she knew no matter what happened she would always have sweet memories of their two tours together.

Forcing herself back to reality she turned towards the airport. Following the skycap inside she went to the group desk and began checking her passengers in for the flight back to Chicago. The "War Department" ladies were on her flight. They immediately started hollering at her about their seat assignments. She tried to calm them down but could hardly wait until she could get back to Chicago and get rid of them.

The agent at the group counter could see she was being harassed by those women. When she got the last of her travelers checked in, it was her turn. He asked her if she wanted to sit in a different section than her passengers. There were two seats on each of the side aisles and he gave her that area to sit in. She told him she could not thank him enough for what he was doing for her. He made a comment about people in the same business sticking together.

When she boarded the plane there was only one person sitting next to her, and he read the entire flight. She was glad she did not have to talk to anyone.

She spent the next four hours thinking about what had just happened to her. She could not believe she had let her guard down like that, even if just for a few moments. She knew she had been so overwhelmed emotionally by several things Chase had said to her.

She also knew her life was going to change for the better due to the profound affect he had upon her. The impact of their meeting and the things he had said would touch her always. She hoped someday she would see him again, if only just to tell him how he had affected her.

She truly hoped he would be happy in his world and that he and his girlfriend would start having fun again. She hated thinking of him being so lonely.

Chapter Sixteen

Once again Nikki was back in Milwaukee. This time she had nine days before her next round of tours when she would be gone for twenty-two days. She would be in the desert for the first trip and then the mountains in September, so packing would be a challenge.

One suitcase was needed just for her tour supplies. She decided to take three suitcases since she needed clothes for the different climates. She always hated it when she had to struggle with three suitcases but knew it could not be helped.

She thought about Chase and wondered what had happened between him and his girlfriend, if anything. She still was not very hungry and when she did eat usually it consisted of lots of fruits and vegetables and fish. She had been eating so much seafood while out on the coast that she now craved it.

She also continued her walking. Actually by mid afternoon, if she put on her earphones and walked down by the lake for about an hour, she found her irritation with Ted would ease quite a bit.

Chase had told her he owned a Harley and that weekend was the one hundredth Harley Davidson birthday rally in Milwaukee. Jay Leno had even come to tape a segment on the birthday bash. There were thousands of bikers all over downtown and traffic was gridlock. Walking was the only option for getting around.

As she walked through the downtown she noticed the bikers. Many of them had on white undershirts, like Chase wore, or black T-shirts. No matter how many bikers she looked at, she could not find a single one who looked as good in an undershirt as Chase had.

She thought of the phrase "absence makes the heart grow fonder..." and told herself to get over it. She knew she was thinking about him because she had such an unsatisfying life with Ted.

For over four years all she had gotten from her husband were those quick kisses on the cheek and the occasional pat on the back. She no longer believed in fairy tales or happy endings, but thanks to Chase, she knew the world could be a happy place if you stayed positively focused on that idea.

Always feeling that "things were meant to be" for a particular reason, she did not know why he had come into her life. There was an email that was forwarded around from time to time about people coming into your life for a reason, a season, or a lifetime. She felt Chase probably fit the first two categories. She also knew she had to stop thinking about him and get on with her life.

Chapter Seventeen

It was not long before she was on her way again. This time the plane was taking her to Las Vegas for the National Parks of the Southwest tour. There would be two nights at the north rim of the Grand Canyon before continuing to the Utah parks that were so spectacular-- Bryce, Zion, and Arches to name some of them.

This was another tour she had been on for the first time last year. It had turned into a favorite trip very quickly and since many of the tour managers would request this tour each year she knew she had been lucky to get assigned to it again.

The previous year she had gotten a wonderful driver named Sam. She had requested him again this year and when she got to the airport to pick up her passengers, she discovered her request had been granted. It was one less thing to worry about on a tour if you already knew the driver and got along well with him.

She had a wealthy group from a large travel club in New Jersey on her tour as well as several individual travelers. There would be close to fifty people she would be in charge of. Her big group was coming in late in the afternoon since their plane had been delayed at Newark.

Arriving in the luggage area she waited for her first passengers. To her delight, not only were the two ladies from her first Pacific Coast trip coming down the escalator, but she also saw four other travelers she had on previous trips. She knew that would help make the tour fun right from the beginning.

Her first priority was getting the passengers gathered up and onto the bus with Sam. She was worried about getting back in time for her next group arrival, so she decided to stay at the airport. After a quick briefing, she let everyone know when she would be back and how to get in contact with her when she returned to the hotel in case they had any questions or concerns. Then she had Sam take the first group of travelers to the hotel before coming back to the airport for her and the travel club group.

She was not sure what the New Jersey people would be like. Actually she and Ted had lived in New Jersey for two years early in their marriage. Her second son, who was now twenty-seven, had been born in that state.

Her main concern was how remote and uncivilized some of the areas they were traveling to would be. When they left Vegas, within an hour she would no longer have cell phone service until they returned on the last day of the tour.

The north rim of the Grand Canyon was her favorite. Only ten percent of the people who visited the Grand Canyon went to the north rim. It was very unspoiled but the cabins were definitely rustic and primitive to say the least. And naturally there was no television.

She remembered trying to explain to some men on a Yellowstone trip in September once, why they would not be able to see Monday night football when they were staying at Old Faithful Lodge.

Her company called it pre-selling. You had to convince the passengers that this was the reason they came to these areas. If there were all the modern conveniences, not only would it spoil the natural beauty, but also it would create a lot of pollution which could eventually affect the park.

Tonight the passengers would be staying at the Golden Nugget, a four star hotel, on Fremont Street. What a difference a day would make! The Grand Canyon cabins were the most primitive rooms on the tour. After that stay the lodging would greatly improve.

After gathering the New Jersey group and getting them on the coach she welcomed them and then briefed them on their free evening. She also gave them a little preview of what would be happening the next day. The coach would be ready to leave Vegas by 8:30 a.m.

The passengers seemed to be in an excellent frame of mind which was usually the case. She just hoped they would stay happy. Usually she found if the travelers were told ahead of time what to expect, they tended to be more open to any UFE's that might occur.

She used the word UFE frequently in her travels. A UFE— Unforgettable Experience-- could be a positive or negative experience. Whether it was a flat tire on the coach or meeting some famous person on a trip, UFE's were something that years later the travelers would still be talking about. You would often hear passengers saying, "Remember that trip we were on ten years ago when... happened?" To Nikki that was a UFE.

She passed out maps of the Vegas area and answered questions from her passengers, including how to take the city bus to the strip. She got her big group checked into the hotel and went back to her room to rest for a little while. She still had to go down to the north tower lobby at 6:00 p.m. to meet and answer questions from the other individual passengers whom she had not yet met; as well as any of the other tour members she had already met who might show up with additional questions.

Finally it was 6:30 p.m. and she was free for the evening. Immediately crossing the street to the Horseshoe Casino, she headed for the twenty-four hour lunch counter located inside. She was planning to have what was becoming her favorite sandwich—tuna fish.

As she ate her sandwich she thought about her travelers. The New Jersey people seemed like a really great group and she already had good vibes that this tour would turn out to be a lot of fun.

Chapter Eighteen

Leaving Las Vegas the next day there were a few clouds in the sky since it was still the rainy season. Several people commented on the humidity in the air. But at least Vegas was experiencing a cool down for early September. It was only going to be in the low ninety's that day. The cooler temperatures would really help since she had planned lunch outside.

The first stop was St. George, Utah for their morning break. A lot of retirees came to this town which had been Brigham Young's winter home. The city was close to the Nevada border for gambling and the climate was so temperate in the winter, the population had been increasing every year. She liked to stop at a grocery store in St. George for her morning break. This way the travelers could buy any needed supplies for their trip. And this would be where she could buy the food for their picnic lunch.

After this stop they were go to Pipe Springs National Monument. Last year there had been a Native American couple running a restaurant near the grounds of the Monument. However one of the tour managers, who had already done the tour this year, told her the restaurant had closed down. The problem was the nearest town was ten miles passed the monument. If she took the passengers to lunch in town they would not get there until 1:30 p.m.

Usually the national parks reserved tables of four in groups of sixteen starting at 5:00 p.m. and continuing every fifteen minutes until everyone in the group had eaten. In that way they did not have to try and serve fifty plus people at once. There was no way she wanted to eat lunch at 1:30 p.m. when the first seating for dinner would begin at 5:00 p.m. Therefore she decided to try a picnic.

She had asked Sam to bring his cooler on the tour. At the grocery store she bought lunchmeat, bread, chips, cookies and water. She also bought paper plates, napkins and ice. It was a little bit of a challenge since she was buying a picnic lunch for fifty people and she only had a half hour to purchase the food.

Her travelers had each given her five dollars for the picnic food. When lunch was finished she still had so many chips, pretzels and cookies left the passengers snacked on the goodies for the next four days. The picnic was a great success and all of them felt they got their money's worth. It had been a very simple lunch but at the end of the tour she still heard travelers talking about the picnic lunch and the fun it had been.

The nicest thing about lunch was it helped everyone to bond. Sitting at picnic tables in small groups, helped introduce people to each other. By the time her travelers left Pipe Springs, they were laughing and talking as if they were old friends.

The elevation at the north rim is 8200 feet—1,200 feet higher than the south rim. Because of this, it is always much cooler at the north rim. By the time they got there the temperature was only in the low sixty's. Everyone went to their cabins and put on much warmer clothes.

Nikki loved being at the north rim. She found a chair right outside the door of the lodge overlooking the canyon and started talking to her passengers whom were sitting there. The two days spent at the north rim gave her a chance to interact with all her travelers in small groups and it was a great way to get to know one another in a relaxed setting.

This afternoon was very special on the rim. They could see rain on the east side of the canyon and after it stopped, a double rainbow appeared.

Nikki and Sam went to the last group dinner seating of the evening. As the waiter brought them their menu, he asked if they wanted a drink with dinner. A beer with her salmon sounded good.

As she perused the drink menu she saw Hefeweizen beer on the list. She ordered one, with a slice of lemon, and when the bottle came she looked at the label. It said Seattle on it. She had not really thought about Chase until that moment. She had been so busy since the trip began, but looking at the bottle made her smile at the memories of being in the sports bar with him.

After dinner she again went outside to sit. She met Jack, one of her passengers from Connecticut. As they watched the sunset, lightening could be seen across the canyon at the south rim. It was almost as if nature was putting on a special show that day. Who needed TV? The movie tonight was called, "Scenery."

The next afternoon, she went on a two-hour mule ride along the rim with some of her passengers. She had wanted to take the half-day ride down into the canyon, but some of her travelers had asked her to do the outing with them since they were afraid to go without her.

As much as she wanted to do the longer ride, it worked out okay because when she got back from her jaunt, there was plenty of time to walk Angel trail. This was something she had never done before and she was looking forward to the experience.

The trail was very challenging and because of the altitude she had to stop and rest several times. She felt a sense of accomplishment walking the trail since she knew she was doing things physically that she had not been able to do the previous year. She was definitely getting in much better shape. She knew if she kept the exercise up she would have no trouble climbing the stairs in her condo.

The next morning they left the north rim. As they were leaving one of the men from New Jersey told her he could not take another day there. He said he was just about to go stir crazy in his small cabin with no amenities. He also told her he would not have missed the experience for anything!

Hearing this type of comment from her travelers made her job seem so worthwhile and rewarding. She also knew this man would have memories of his tour that he would talk about and treasure for the rest of his life.

Chapter Nineteen

The rest of the tour went well and her travelers were having a wonderful time. Many of these people had traveled all over the world but had never been to any of the Western states.

Nikki and Sam were so accustomed to the West and tended to forget how awed everyone from the East Coast were by the wide-open spaces. She knew that for the next few days her passengers would continue to be wowed by the sights.

They continued on to Moab, Utah for two nights. The following day would be a tour of Arches National Park with a local guide and a river-rafting trip down the Colorado River.

The evening dinner was an on your own meal. Last year she had gone to a restaurant about a block from the hotel and had eaten alone. This time she asked Sam where he was having dinner. He mentioned a Mexican restaurant about two blocks away.

Since none of her travelers would be going to that restaurant and after her experiences with Chase, she readily agreed to go with Sam when he invited her. It was definitely more fun than eating alone. Her driver was very happily married and she knew they would have a good time together talking about different road adventures they had been on.

Yesterday held many sweet memories for her and she was not interested in anymore lonely todays. Besides taking care of her body she knew she needed to rethink her life emotionally. She finally realized "fun" was not going to come knocking on her door. She had to go out in search of it. And as long as she set boundaries with her drivers as Chase had suggested, there was no reason for her not to eat with them.

There were many more wonderful sights ahead. One of her favorite was Bryce Canyon, described as the most colorful park in the world. The red, pink, and orange colors in the "hoodoo" rocks that stood one thousand feet tall never failed to amaze her.

Today the passengers were in for a real treat. Usually she would walk the travelers the half-mile walk on the rim between Sunset and Sunrise Point. When the coach arrived at Sunset Point it was cloudy and drizzling a little. But by the time they had walked half way to Sunrise Point the sun came out. She let her passengers know how lucky they had been to observe the different colors of the rocks with the clouds and then how different the colors in the rocks looked in the sun.

Bryce is also dotted with the deep greens of ponderosa pines and ancient bristle cone pines. Chase had told her a lot of information about bristle cone pine trees that she had not known before. As they walked along the rim of the canyon she began explaining the differences in the trees to some of her passengers. She was also able to point them out so they could distinguish the two types of trees up close.

One of her favorite trees was the ponderosa pine. Many local guides said the older trees had a butterscotch smell. However she thought the trees smelled more like vanilla. The next thing she knew several of her passengers were "hugging the ponderosa pines." Others were taking pictures and several were trying to determine if the trees smelled of butterscotch or vanilla. Most agreed with Nikki.

These were the kind of moments that made the trips so unique to her. This passing thought reminded her of how delighted the passengers had been to see the Oregon lighthouse she and Chase had taken them to.

After Bryce they continued to Springdale for a two-night stay in the Zion National Park area. The next morning they had a guided tour of the park and then had some free time before Sam came back in the coach to pick them up.

She had heard of some trails across the street from the lodge that were supposed to be pretty interesting. Naturally last year she had never attempted to even find a trail more less hike one. Although the temperature was in the nineties she put on her hat, filled her bottle of water and crossed the street for her walk.

The trail she chose was mostly uphill but she realized climbing was definitely getting easier for her. She never stopped to rest until she got to the end of the trail and was starting her return back down.

That evening was their "farewell dinner." She was really going to miss her passengers. She had met some wonderful people on this tour. She knew the travelers would have wonderful memories of their trip but she would also have great memories of the people she had met.

One man in particular she really liked. He was a real sweetheart and had a wonderful sense of humor. Every day he found something to laugh about. His wife had told her he was very sick and so she had tried to do some things to make the tour easier for him.

It would be many months later when she received a note from his wife saying how the extra things she had done for him had meant so much to both of them. They knew he was dying when they came on the trip and he only lived six weeks after their return home.

His wife mentioned in her note how he spent his last moments telling everyone what an amazing vacation he had been on and how much the tour manager had done for him to make the trip that much more enjoyable. He had been in a lot of pain most of the time but all the laughter he and Nikki had shared had made him look forward to each new day being on the tour.

That letter brought tears to her. She was so glad she had been able to ease his pain a little. But it also made her a little sad that for some reason she was not able to reach her husband in any positive way as she was capable of doing with her travelers. She also realized all the positive comments she received from her passengers helped her self confidence. This was so important since living with Ted did nothing to reinforce her self worth.

Chapter Twenty

Back to back time…

Nikki and Sam got all their passengers dropped off at their various airlines at the Las Vegas airport. She and her driver had really worked well as a team, as they had the previous year and had fun together at the same time.

Sam had done several trips to Yellowstone with another tour company that summer. Other drivers from his charter bus company had been handling her company's National Park tours. However she had sent in her request for Sam, and like Chase, he decided even though he could make more money with the other tour companies, it was nice to have a change of pace. And he especially wanted to do it since he liked working with her. Saying good-bye at the airport, he said, "Maybe you could do two of these trips next year." That statement made her smile.

She liked it when drivers looked forward to working with her. It made it so much easier when you had a driver you could depend on and trust. She liked to tease her returning drivers and tell them how much she enjoyed having them "broken in."

Little did she guess what was about to happen next. She had never considered writing up a driver. She knew this was their livelihood. Besides there was only one time in six years that she had not liked her driver. It was her first year as a tour manager and that particular man had kept getting lost even though the directions were written on the itinerary.

The worst was when he got on the interstate the wrong way after a morning break and they had to travel eight miles in the wrong direction before they could find an exit to turn around. She suspected he was sneaking booze, although she could never prove it. When she got back and told her boss what had happened, he called the coach office and the man never drove for her company again.

Having been so busy having fun with her passengers and Sam, she had not thought of Chase since the Hefeweizen beer at the Grand Canyon. But as she walked down the concourse at the airport in Vegas there was a remembrance. Right in front of her was a Starbucks!

It was ironic how when she least expected it something would remind her of him. It made her a little sad that she had no way to contact him. Many of her drivers had email and it was nice to keep in touch with them from time to time. She hoped that someday Chase would drag himself into the 21st century since he had neither email nor a cell phone!

Her plane left Vegas at 1:30 p.m. for Denver. She had a one-hour time change and it was 6:00 p.m. by the time she got into her hotel room. Since she was pretty worn out after her National Parks trip she went next door from the hotel to a sandwich shop. She ordered a turkey sandwich to bring back to her room.

By the time she opened her suitcases, ate her sandwich, and had a bath, she decided she was no longer able to think. She quickly fell asleep by 8:00 p.m., knowing she would feel fresher in the morning and could get an early start.

Once again she would be meeting new people in

her life and a new adventure lay ahead. This time she would be taking five different trains across Colorado. This was the only tour she had ever been on when the men at the end of the trip would leave with tears in their eyes.

Chapter Twenty-One

Riding the hotel shuttle to the airport she was once again on her way to gather up her travelers. After getting everyone's suitcases, she let ground transportation know they were ready. Then her coach was sent from the holding area to pick everyone up.

As the driver got off the bus she saw an older very heavyset man. He seemed jovial enough as he loaded the luggage in the bay. He told her his name was Dean.

Since his company was Denver based the driver did not stay at the hotel with the passengers and tour manager. She told him they needed to leave at 8:00 a.m. the next morning and he responded that he would be there at 7:00 a.m. to get the luggage loaded. After dropping them off at the hotel he left for home.

She spent the next few hours with her travelers, including a welcome dinner. She had a large group from Washington State and there was a group leader who had been sent to make sure her passengers were well taken care of.

Mary, the group leader, told her that her husband also drove motor coaches. At that point some of Mary's passengers mentioned how obsessive her husband was about keeping his coach clean. This made Nikki smile. Both Chase and her friend Max, an Illinois driver, were up at 5:00 a.m. making sure everything on the coach was clean for the day, including spotless windows. She knew she would like Mary's husband if she ever met him.

The day went pretty smoothly. Dean was early and loaded the luggage. He seemed to joke often and at one point told her, "I'll grow on you." For some reason this comment rubbed her the wrong way but she just let it go.

The other thing that bothered her about her driver was every chance he could take he would be standing by the door of the coach smoking a cigarette! Not only did she not like this, but she also knew the tour members would soon start complaining about the smoke to her. She mentioned to him that he might want to move farther away from the door when smoking. He actually gave her a nasty look!

Dean would not be riding on any of the trains but rather deadheading. This meant he would take the bus to the furthest point the train went to. In this way the group would not have to return to where the train started, and they could keep moving throughout the state.

Their first stop was Colorado Springs and Pike's Peak. She was not looking forward to being on the top of Pike's Peak. She had warned her passengers of altitude sickness, including the fact that they needed to drink plenty of water. She had even gone to the little store next to the Denver hotel and purchased two cases of water so all her travelers would have a bottle to begin the first train ride with. Since they would be over 14,000 feet thin air could definitely be a problem; especially since they had not had time to acclimate to the altitude.

The previous year she had two passengers need oxygen while at the top. And she had also felt very dizzy even though she had drunk a lot of water. To her amazement this year she felt fine at the top. She had probably gotten used to higher altitudes somewhat after being 8,000 feet up at the Grand Canyon. She also thought all her walking and exercising was helping, too.

After their ride to the top of Pike's Peak Dean drove them to dinner. As he got to their destination he pulled up across the street from the restaurant. As he stopped the coach she told him he could pull over into the restaurant parking lot.

Very brusquely he told her he could not get into the lot. She was a little surprised and told him all the other coaches she had been on previously on this tour had pulled into that particular lot for drop off. He told her in no uncertain terms he was staying right where he was.

There was no way she was going to make an issue out of this in front of her passengers. All she wanted to do was get everyone into the restaurant for dinner. However as she looked out the front of the window she saw a big puddle of water. "At least pull up past the puddle so the travelers don't get their feet wet." He did as she asked but acted very sullen with the request.

His actions reminded her of her driver friend Max from Illinois. They had done many trips together and he had once told her he did not believe there was a driver in the world she could not get along with. She had a bad feeling she had just met one.

As she walked everyone across the street the restaurant manager came out to greet her. The first thing she told her was how dangerous it was to park where they had since it was such a busy street. She recommended the driver pull into the lot. She told the woman she was aware of the conditions but her driver had refused to pull in. The manager just shook her head as she and Nikki walked into the restaurant.

Once again she was reminded of Chase when they had been in Portland. One night as they walked from the

Italian restaurant back to the hotel he had pointed out his bus which was parked on the busy one-way street in front of the hotel.

"See how the back of my bus is sticking out from the curb?"

"Yes."

"Do you know why I do that?"

"I don't have a clue."

"I park that way because when the cars come quickly around the corner they have to make a wide swing or run into the back of me. By making the wide swing they are far enough into the street that the passengers climbing on the coach will not get hurt since the door is on the street side."

"Wow, that is pretty neat." Chase had smiled at her proud of himself that she realized how much he cared about his passengers. It was too bad Dean could not be thoughtful like that to the travelers.

The next morning they were getting ready to leave Colorado Springs. As she walked through the coach counting people she noticed the floor did not look as if it had been swept.

Some drivers, like Max and Chase, could be obsessive about keeping their coach clean which she actually liked. However all drivers did the basics, including sweeping the floor every night. She thought perhaps Dean planned to sweep while they were on the train ride since they had gotten in late the evening before.

As she continued counting, one of the travelers stopped her. "Nikki, there are still two pieces of luggage with our baggage tags upstairs." She looked at the woman with a shocked expression. As she boarded the coach that morning she had asked Dean if his luggage count was correct—forty-eight pieces--and he had said "yes."

Tour managers are responsible for luggage.

However, the driver's job was to count the luggage as well as take the bags on and off the bus. She had been touring for six years and never had a problem with bags. Of course that meant trusting that the driver did his part.

"Are you sure," she asked the passenger? "What floor were the suitcases on," she continued since the hotel had four floors?

"We saw them towards the back of the hotel on the second floor."

Going up to Dean he once again reconfirmed he had his correct luggage count. She told him she needed to go back into the hotel to check on something. She noticed as soon as she went inside he also got off the bus so he could smoke another cigarette.

As she walked down the hallway of the second floor she saw two pieces of luggage with the blue tags her company always used sitting next to a door. She was so mad she could hardly see straight. She picked up the two bags and carried them down the stairs. She took them and dropped them by Dean's feet as he continued smoking.

"Obviously your count was off."

"I thought I had the right count."

He did not even look upset and never said he was sorry. She had a feeling things were going to get worse. Her passengers were having a wonderful time and had no idea what was going on and that was the way she wanted it. The only problem with back-to-back tours was no time to recharge. She was worried about getting through another five days with this driver. Thank goodness she was able to have some time away from him while riding the trains. She was trying very hard not to lose her cool in front of him.

His sloppy behavior continued. Each day the floor was worse than the day before and one could hardly see out the windows with all the bugs and dirt. Then another problem developed.

Drivers never spoke on the microphone unless a tour manager would ask them to say something. Dean had a microphone right in front of his mouth. Obviously his Denver Company used a lot of driver guides and this was a way for the driver to speak while driving.

After the trip began he got on the microphone and started to tell jokes and stories. He constantly interrupted her and many times the passengers would not understand his punch line after a particularly long story. She had the feeling he was trying to make it look like she did not know the area well with all his little "insights." It was obvious he was doing his best to put her down in an insidious manner.

He also continued to park quite a distance away wherever they stopped, and she knew neither Max, Chase, nor any other driver she had ever had would have done that. Dropping passengers as close as possible to the places where they stopped was something all drivers tried to do. One day they even ran into another bus from Dean's company and that driver was dropping his people right at the front door of the building while they parked at the far end of the lot.

The thing that bothered her the most was the dirty windows. There were so many bugs it was hard to see the spectacular sights out the windows. The front window was divided into fourths and she asked Dean several times to clean that window. However whenever she came back to the coach only the section in front of him had been washed.

On the last day she had been on the road twenty-two days and was ready to go home. When Dean dropped them at the airport she told him she would go get a skycap. She wanted the travelers to stay on the coach until she had all the pieces of luggage unloaded.

Denver was another airport that was a challenge with the coach parking. She would have to walk the passengers up another level for check in so she wanted to make sure all the luggage was on the carts so it would arrive upstairs when they did.

As she returned to the coach with her skycap she noticed he had all the luggage unloaded by the curb. He also had all the passengers standing on the busy sidewalk waiting for her return.

Dean was sitting at the wheel inside the bus. She gathered up her travelers, and not even giving him a glance, walked into the terminal. As he drove off she realized he was the first driver in her career that she never said good-bye to.

Chapter Twenty-Two

Back in Wisconsin she only had six days before she would fly back to Denver for another train trip. The next tour would be a challenge because she had fifty-two passengers and her company would also have a special group there at the same time in three other coaches.

She had only turned in the one previous driver who kept getting lost to her company for incompetence. She knew this could affect their job status. However she felt Dean was totally unacceptable to any other tour manager in her company to have to put up with. She knew the three coach move passengers were very important clients for her company. If one of those coaches got Dean and had to go through what she had, they would be very angry with her for not reporting him.

So she wrote everything up in her reports but then thought about it for a day. She realized no one would see the reports for a couple more days. Because of that she emailed the head of transportation at her company.

One of her bosses called her back. He was extremely upset. He said what she went through was totally unacceptable. He was mad at her for not calling sooner. He felt the driver should have been replaced in the middle of the tour. That made her smile since she knew that would not happen during a trip unless something much worse occurred.

Her main concern had been if she had let her company know earlier what was going on and Dean's company had called him with her report, things might have gotten worse for her while she was still on the road with him. She was proud of the fact that his behavior had not affected any of her tour members.

In fact only one person came up to her and said anything during the tour. The group leader whose husband was a driver spoke to her early on. She told her, she knew exactly what was happening. She tried to brush her comments off but felt a little better knowing someone else knew what she was going through.

At least it was over now and she knew that neither she nor the other three tour managers would have to worry about getting Dean as a driver on their next tour.

Since there were only a few days before her next journey, she was extremely busy getting reports and papers ready and making calls. She noticed her pants were getting pretty baggy but she did not have time to go shopping.

Since her pants had elastic bands she would just have to make do. Not having a scale she assumed she was probably losing a little weight from all her exercising and eating properly. She suddenly realized she had not had a dessert since her trip with Chase. However she did not feel she was missing anything even though desserts came with every included meal. She was thinking she would have to buy some new pants when she returned from this next tour.

The next adventure went extremely well, especially considering it ended up being a four-coach move. There were a few challenges since all four coaches had to ride the trains at the same time. However she and the other tour managers got along very well and made adjustments as necessary, so they did not run into each other at shopping or rest stops.

When she got back to Wisconsin she knew it was definitely time to buy some new pants. She had a trip to Myrtle Beach, South Carolina in eight days and none of her clothes fit.

There was a health club down the street and she walked over there to ask if she could check her weight on their scale. Wow was she in for a shock. In a little less than two months, she had taken off almost twenty-five pounds! No wonder none of her clothes fit. When she went to the store she found she had gone down three pants sizes!

Nikki was thrilled to say the least. She never expected to lose that much weight especially since she was not really trying to diet. She just knew she felt so much better.

When she arrived home from the department store, she put on a new pair of jeans—sized ten--and tucked her shirt in. As she glanced at the size sixteen pants in her closet she was sure her husband would notice. However he never once said a word to her about the way she looked!

She had not been at this new weight in fifteen years. She continued her hourly walks to the lake every day. Ted was still stressing her out and it helped her get through the day. Everyone she knew who ran into her commented on the weight loss, which made her feel even better. Everyone that is except Ted!

Over the next few weeks she continued with her tours. Her scores were extremely high and she knew this was going to be a year to remember. She even took off a few more pounds which made her clothes fit even better. Still there was not a word from her husband about her weight loss although everyone else she ran into commented about how she looked.

One night they were out to dinner with another couple that was visiting from out of town. Their friends immediately commented about how she looked.

"You lost weight," Ted asked?

"Not that you would notice, Ted. Obviously I am invisible to you."

"That's not true. I just don't see well."

In more ways than one she thought to herself.

The next day she was leaving once again for another tour.

"Tell me if you lose anymore weight, Nikki."

Knowing he was upset about the invisible remark she had made in front of their friends did not even bother her. She was finding it very hard to care about any of her husband's wants or feelings. Even though he now knew about the weight loss he still had not said she looked good.

Shaking her head as she left for her tour she knew she was quickly reaching the end of her rope. They had been married close to thirty-two years but she did not know if she could take much more. His selfish desire to only focus on himself was getting to her.

It was almost the end of October and this would be her last tour until after Thanksgiving when she would be doing two Christmas trips to San Antonio's River walk.

As she got in her car she put her cup on the dash. She had a large sized insulated cup she used for coffee. She thought it was ugly but took it everywhere. Now she noticed it had a crack running along the bottom.

She had not thought of Chase in awhile. All of a sudden she remembered their last tour the morning they were in Eureka. She had been sitting in a chair in the lobby waiting for the manager to make sure everything was alright with her bill.

Chase was standing next to her and asked her what had happened to her cup? She thought the cup was on the table beside her but when she looked it was not there.

Since she had gone outside for a newspaper, thinking she might have left it on top of the newspaper container, she quickly went out to look.

However it was not there. As she came back in the cup was on the table right next to the lobby chair she had been sitting in. She suddenly realized he had hidden her cup. She smiled at him and said a prayer she would do another tour with him next year. Some morning he would probably find his latte missing if they did another tour together.

She also thought of her Illinois driver, Max. Max was forty-four and a real sweet man. He would do anything for her or the passengers. She used to tease him and tell him he would give the shirt off his back to his worst enemy.

The first three trips with Max, she had always spilled her coffee on his clean floor even though she tried to brace her cup. She felt bad for messing up his floor but also because she had to go without coffee until the morning break. He told her if they ever got to Nebraska he was going to have her get a new cup.

The very next year they were doing a trip to Laughlin together. When they got to Nebraska they stopped at a truck stop. He told her to follow him in. He went to a shelf and said, "There, buy that cup." She picked it up and thought how ugly it was. However there was a big piece of rubber on the bottom of the cup. She knew she would never spill her coffee again. Naturally she had bought the cup. And the cup had been on every trip with her since.

Her last tour during the fall season went down Route 66 and eventually into Las Vegas for four nights. The trip went well and she was sad when it ended. Now she had a month of dealing with her husband and his complaints. She emailed her brother Randy. She still had her two holiday San Antonio tours but she wondered if they should not plan a cruise for Christmas or New Year's.

Chapter Twenty-Three

Checking her email there was some devastating news from Max. He had gone in for a check-up because he had been having pain in his shoulders. The doctor had told him he had stage four-lung cancer!

There were several "hot spots." They could not operate or give him radiation because the cancer was too advanced. They could give him some chemo to help shrink the tumors. He only had nine months to live but the chemo might give him a little longer if he decided to go for that treatment.

Her first thought was it could not be true. He was too young for this to be happening. Then she remembered her cracked cup and shivered when she realized she had noticed the crack about the time Max was being diagnosed.

Her troubles with Ted seemed inconsequential compared to what Max would now be going through. She called him that weekend and reminisced about all their journeys together. She was surprised when he told her she needed to start living.

Max was the only driver who knew some of the problems she was experiencing with her husband. They had been traveling together for so many years; it was hard for him not to know a little about her life. Usually she did not mention much about Ted to her drivers. However

Max had done some tours with her when he had been in contact with Ted and had seen how he acted around her. Although they had never discussed anything too personal Max decided to speak up because of his circumstances.

"Nikki you can never count on how much time you have left in this life. You need to have fun. Don't let your husband's negativism beat you down."

It was extremely rare for the two of them to go out since Ted preferred staying at home. Sometimes she found herself in her house with no one to talk to for days on end. Many of their former friends had moved from their area and with the type of work she did it was hard to meet new people. That is why she looked forward to her tours and meeting new people.

She could not believe this was the second person in just a few months to tell her to have fun.

She remembered Chase saying "it wasn't fun anymore." If he only knew how true that remark was for her. She knew couples did not need to have everything in common. Sometimes differences could make a relationship more interesting. However she decided right then and there if she ever had a chance for another relationship in her lifetime, it would be with a fun sensitive man who she enjoyed being with and who enjoyed being with her. Otherwise she would walk away as fast as she could.

If something happened to her husband, she felt she would never remarry. She never again wanted someone to have that kind of power over her or feel forced into a role of housekeeper/mother. She had seen quite a few passengers on her coaches who were happily married for a second time, but she did not think that was in the cards for her.

What sounded better to her was a no strings, no commitment, either short or long-term sexual relationship with someone she knew and trusted and who she could talk to. She wanted a man who would want to do little things for her just to make her happy. And she would reciprocate. And she wanted to laugh. She remembered all the times Chase made her laugh and how good it made her feel.

The only way a relationship could be good was if there was good communication. As Mama Gena said: "couples were not mind readers." Sometimes small slights turned into big problems because of some statement misinterpreted by the other. She had seen that happen with her friends and had felt sad when they had let something very small become so big they had broken up.

This was not true in her case. Ted's strokes had caused an imbalance in his brain and he just did not know how to communicate normally anymore. He had always been selfish but it seemed the stroke had made all his flaws much more pronounced. And she decided she did not want to quit living just because her husband had.

Randy, her brother, came for a visit and the first thing he said to her was, "my, we are looking nice and thin." This comment made her smile. She could not remember how many years it had been since Ted had said something nice like that to her. She told her brother about some of her new thoughts.

Randy totally agreed with her.

"Nikki, the operative word for next year is going to be FUN!"

You can be married to Ted and still have fun. Or maybe you will decide to divorce. She was shocked by her brother's comment. She had not really thought about divorce before and was surprised he mentioned it.

"It's not really that bad, Randy."

"It's worse than you think, Nikki."

Worried that her husband would totally give up on life if she left him, made this an option she was not willing to consider. But then she also remembered Ted's doctor telling her she had to quit feeling guilty for choices her husband was making. She knew she felt very conflicted and was not sure what she wanted anymore.

She was feeling so much better about herself, especially with all the positive comments she was receiving. In addition what was happening to Max was making her rethink what she wanted from life.

Mentioning the cruise to Randy, he thought it was an excellent idea.

"We can go dance or listen to music and if Ted wants to stay in his room we will just leave him there Nikki."

Once again she was reminded of what Chase had said about meeting and just talking to people on a cruise. She wondered if she could do that. She did it all the time with her job so why not on a cruise.

She and Randy got on the Internet and found a five day New Year's cruise out of Galveston, Texas that was fairly reasonable. They booked it right then and there.

Chapter Twenty-Four

Time passed quickly. It always seemed to do that during the holidays. Ted and Nikki's sons and her brother Randy spent Thanksgiving together. Her two San Antonio tours, the last of her trips for the year, went well and she knew she would remember this tour season with fondness. She had many passengers emailing or writing her. They wanted her to keep them informed of her upcoming trips.

Her sons were in their late twenties and not married. Christmas did not hold the appeal for any of them as when there were children around.

They all decided to spend Christmas together in New Orleans. It was a fun city and they were able to get a four star hotel very reasonably since this was not a high tourist time. When Christmas was over their sons would fly home and Nikki, Ted, and Randy would continue on to Galveston. The island was only a few hours away and they would catch their cruise ship there.

They spent the next few days exploring New Orleans. Ted spent a lot of time in the hotel room watching television but for once this did not bother her. She was having fun! And it was probably more so without listening to her husband's constant negative views.

On Christmas Eve they had dinner at a restaurant in the French Quarter a couple of blocks from their hotel.

Ted had gone back to the hotel saying he would pick up a sandwich in the coffee shop. Nikki knew he was upset with Randy and her because they had been laughing so much. Ted truly hated it when he knew people were happy and he kept making snide remarks about their laughing. Before he left them at the restaurant, even their sons were looking at him strangely.

The service at dinner was extremely slow. They did not have a large staff on duty since it was Christmas Eve. Everyone was having such a good time talking and laughing and enjoying each other's company they had not really noticed the slow service. Part of having fun was enjoying the moment.

There was nothing else to do that night except have dinner and talk. They overheard some of the tables near them chiding the waiter. Nikki knew the server was doing his best in a difficult situation and always wondered why people would get so upset over a situation they could not control.

When the waiter came to their table and apologized for the delay she told him not to worry about it, and to take care of the irate diners first. The next thing they knew the manager was at their table with free drinks for all of them. The manager thanked them for their understanding and patience and they thanked him in return for the drinks.

Randy was shocked. "I have been to the French Quarter a few times, and giving out free drinks is not something they do here."

Looking at her brother she nodded and responded, "It is all part of the fun!"

The Christmas vacation was soon over and the boys boarded their flight for home. The three of them drove over to Galveston and checked into their hotel which was situated right on Seawall Boulevard with views of the Gulf of Mexico.

The next day was spent exploring the island. There were so many things to do that she and her brother wished they had an extra day to spend there.

However it was soon time to board the ship for their cruise to Cozumel and Cancun and they were looking forward to that also. They had chosen the early seating for dinner because Ted did not like to eat late. Nikki realized that would give them more time to check out the shows and activities that were going on during the evening hours.

By 9:00 p.m. Ted decided to go to bed. Randy and Nikki went to one of the show rooms to listen to a band. After sitting there a few minutes she decided to leave. The band was a country western band, which her brother liked, but she did not.

Deciding to try out Chase's advice she went and checked out the piano bar. There were a few people sitting around the piano on stools that circled the piano. There was one empty seat in between everyone sitting there. She sat down and ordered a Corona beer with a lime.

The piano player's name was Ken. He had a songbook and people came up by the piano and sang. Although she had never been able to carry a tune she enjoyed listening to the music and to the people who came in try their turn at singing.

This was her first experience with karaoke. Some of the singers were very good and others terrible. She started talking to the couples around her and pretty soon they were all cheering even when the bad singers completed their song. She sat there until the bar closed and could not believe how enjoyable it had been.

The next night Ted wanted to watch movies on television after dinner. Randy went with her to the piano bar. He stayed quite a while but then decided to go listen to the country band again. By this time she was getting to know the names of many of the people in the bar and they knew hers.

There were probably thirty people who would come in and out to sing. There were another ten people who stayed there most of the evening like she did. She could not believe what a good time she was having. She did not mind being there as a single since she felt a part of the whole group and no one tried to hit on her.

New Year's Eve day they docked in Cozumel for the day. Her brother went diving and she spent the day downtown window shopping. About 4:00 p.m. she stopped at one of the waterfront bars and had a Corona.

Sitting and watching the people go by was an interesting experience. For some reason she really did not mind being alone and liked sitting in the tropical surroundings. She knew Ted was spending the day in his cabin watching movies and she was happy for the time away from him.

As she returned to the ship the boat Randy had been on for the diving expedition docked. They walked back on the ship together and started telling each other about their day.

She realized her job definitely helped her feel at ease doing her own thing. Since she often ate alone on her pre tour nights in a new city; being alone was beginning to feel comfortable. Having been married for so long and being "a couple," she had never felt secure as a single. But now she was discovering it was not such a bad thing at all. In fact she was beginning to enjoy her time away from her husband.

Sometimes she felt Ted would follow her around just because he worried she might be having fun without him. Naturally he came to the piano bar that night with her and Randy.

It was New Year's Eve and everyone had been given those noisy horns to blow. After every song Nikki and Randy were blowing their horns. When they asked Ken, the piano player, if he minded them blowing their horns, he said he loved it and so they continued.

Meanwhile her husband was sitting next to her blowing smoke in her face. There was an empty seat around the piano by the wall about six seats down. Nikki asked him to move there to smoke. He complied. The bar closed early that night so all the passengers could go out on deck to the party that would welcome in the New Year. Nikki was so glad they had decided to go on the cruise. With the stars twinkling above them this was certainly a special way to welcome the New Year.

New Year's Day she and her brother were up at 7:00 a.m. They had signed up for an excursion to see some Mayan ruins and then on to a water park lagoon for the afternoon. Once again Ted would spend the day watching movies on television in their cabin since he hated going anywhere.

The ruins were even more spectacular than she imagined. Her brother enjoyed the water park snorkeling and tubing. She did a little tubing too, but decided she much preferred spending time in a hammock watching the dolphin show going on nearby. It had been a perfect day.

On the way back to the ship, the local guide was selling Corona's for two dollars. Most people in the back of the bus were drinking the beer and one man bought a round for ten of them. Their only complaint was no lime!

She was hoping to escape from Ted that evening but the problem was he knew where her "hideout" was. When she entered the piano bar her husband was sitting at the end of the bar in his smoking chair. The piano player asked her where her horn was. She said she had left it her cabin but she could get it.

Ken said, "Do it Nikki." As she reentered the bar with her two horns, her brother showed up. They both began blowing their horns after every song.

Ted leaned over and said, "Randy that is very irritating. Stop it."

This statement infuriated her. He was picking on Randy even though she was also blowing the horn.

Turning to him she said, "If you don't like it then leave." After the next song she noticed her husband was gone.

By this time, she had become friends with several of the people in the bar. They knew each other's names and talked back and forth. When they ran into each other on the ship during the daytime they would also stop and chat.

She wished she could tell Chase how right he had been. She made a silent wish that his life was as good as hers was. Life with Ted was far from perfect but at least she was finally having some fun.

Ken had mentioned coming to teatime the next afternoon. He said the piano playing was very sedate in the afternoon but she told him she and her brother would be there and would liven it up a little. Unfortunately, Ted heard her.

The next day was their last full day on ship. Going up on the deck late in the morning, she went to the walking track. On days at sea she walked about an hour with her headset on. It was a perfect setting for a walk looking at the ocean stretched in front of you on all sides.

Only making it around the deck once, she spotted her brother on the next level above her. She went up to see what he was doing and ask him about going to lunch.

To her surprise he was sitting with the couple that

had bought the beers on the bus on the way back from the ruins the previous day. She sat down for what she thought would be a few minutes. It was just after 11:00 a.m.

The next thing she knew it was 4:00 p.m. and many beers later. She mentioned to Randy they needed to go to teatime since she had promised Ken they would come. Besides they had not eaten lunch and she knew there were sandwiches there.

As they entered the bar she spotted Ted at his smoking place up at the piano with a cup of tea in front of him. She was hoping he would not be there but knew he was probably upset she had been gone all day. She sat four stools down from him. He asked her where she had been and she told him. He could not believe she would not at least have eaten lunch.

"I was having too much fun."

As she was talking to Ken, her husband leaned over the bar and said, "Nikki, get me another cup of tea."

Normally she was careful what she said to him in public. But she could not believe what he had just said. He had managed to get his first cup of tea. Now that she was there she was supposed to wait on him.

Looking at him she said, "Get your own tea. You got your first cup. I am NOT your maid."

She heard a gasp from Ken at the piano. He had been talking to her husband before she came in. Now he quit talking to him at all. Unfortunately Randy went and got Ted another cup of tea. This upset her. She hated the way Ted manipulated people so they would enable him.

Not wanting to create a scene she said nothing. She did not want people to feel sorry for her. At the same time she realized that order had been the final straw. She knew within the next few months she would line up a housekeeper to come in a few hours a day to take care of

Ted. She was going to separate from him. Next summer she was determined to have a different lifestyle.

The last evening in the piano bar found her with all her newfound friends. Randy was listening to the country band. She did not know or care where Ted was, although she guessed he was probably in his room watching a movie.

Overall it had been a wonderful cruise and she hoped maybe she could take another one next New Year's.

Chapter Twenty-Five

January was a pretty uneventful month. She spent a few days in Chicago working at the office and attending her company's yearly meeting. She spoke to her boss while there about her summer schedule.

She had always wanted to spend a summer on the Pacific Coast. In fact the summer after Ted's stroke, he had met her in Seattle when she had two weeks between the tours she was doing out there. They had traveled around the Olympic Peninsula and all the way down the coast of Oregon looking for possible sites to live.

That fall 9/11 took place. She knew national air travel would be down the following summer. Since there would not be enough national tours, living on the Pacific Coast would probably no longer be feasible.

However conditions changed. Her boss told her in January there were many international travelers who were now traveling nationally. This was bringing her company a big surge in national tours. She mentioned to him her desire to go west for the summer. He told her that she would have more work than she needed, if she was living out in the Northwest. It seemed a lot easier to be living closer to her jobs than constantly flying three or four hours one way just to get in place.

She was beginning to think that it was meant for

her to go live some where in either Oregon or Washington. She would love to live on a boat but only time would tell if that would be a possibility.

All thoughts of living on the West Coast were put on the back burner one morning towards the end of January.

Ted awoke with a very bad backache and numbness in his foot. He could hardly stand. She was able to get him an appointment with his doctor for that afternoon. The doctor ordered an MRI. It was a few days before they would get the results, and Ted was given some painkillers to help with the pain.

The following week, she and her husband went to the doctor's office for the report on his back. He had a very serious herniated disc. The doctor thought it might get better. He did not see surgery as an option at that point because Ted's health was so poor.

Naturally her husband did not want surgery. If he did have an operation and needed several weeks or even months to recuperate, she could see all her plans to separate from him go down the drain.

Knowing she should have more sympathy for him was difficult. Even their doctor told her many of his problems were caused by a combination of his smoking and inactivity. He had always felt that if he ignored the problem it would cease to exist. He preferred spending the day sitting on his couch reading his paper with the television on.

The doctor knew her husband was deeply depressed but he absolutely refused to take medicine for his depression. Everything was always about Ted's wants and desires. She wondered when it would be her turn. If she stayed with him, she knew it would never happen.

She thought of a saying one of her friends had told her. "If you want to give God a good laugh, just tell Him your plans." She was beginning to think she would spend the rest of her life tied to Ted's aches and pains but was at a loss as to how to change her situation.

At this point events were out of her hands. She knew she would have to see how things developed and realized she could not force change. All she could do was sit back and let events unfold.

She did not want to worry about what might happen tomorrow. If it did not happen then she would have worried for nothing. And if it did happen, then she would have worried twice. She did not want to borrow from the future. Let the future come to her. There was not a thing she could do to control this event right now anyway.

Her husband was sent to physical therapy and continued taking painkillers. Slowly the pain in his back got better although his foot remained numb. He said it was like he had a boot on all the time. Since he could no longer drive, taking Ted to physical therapy three times a week kept her busy.

One afternoon about four weeks into his therapy Nikki became upset with her husband. Ted never did any of the follow up exercises the therapist prescribed on the days he was not with her. She had a feeling he was wasting his time and money going through the motions of physical therapy.

It was very difficult feeling bad about his pain when he did not seem to care about helping himself. When she told him as much he just laughed at her and told her to leave him alone. He was content with the way things were. She just shrugged and felt frustrated that nothing ever changed. She truly felt trapped in a hopeless situation.

Before long, March arrived. Having been assigned a tour to Las Vegas she felt Ted was well enough for her to leave him. She arranged for a lady to come and spend four hours a day with him fixing his food and straightening up the place. The woman would also take him to his physical therapy although Nikki felt it was becoming a total waste of time.

She was extremely excited about the tour. The day she drove out of the garage headed for the first coach pick up stop, she felt as if a giant weight had been lifted from her. She felt free for the first time in weeks. At times she felt a little guilty about feeling so euphoric leaving her husband. But she also realized that for her own mental health she needed the break. And besides once again a new adventure and new people awaited her.

Chapter Twenty-Six

There were signs of spring everywhere as Nikki's motor coach traveled down Route 66 on her twelve-day trip from Wisconsin to Las Vegas. They were spending four nights in Las Vegas at the Golden Nugget on Fremont Street. Her company liked that hotel. They got a good rate and it was a four-star hotel right downtown.

Most of Nikki's passengers were seniors and it was much easier directing them around the Fremont Street area than out on the strip. Besides, there was so much less walking involved for her older travelers.

The second full day in Vegas was a free day for Nikki. There would be an evening show but otherwise she had some time to call her own.

Sleeping in for a change she had a nice breakfast buffet at the hotel since it was an included meal. After breakfast she went wandering in the gift shops that lined Fremont Street. She wanted to buy some cheap trinkets as prizes for the games she would play on the coach. She also needed to buy some birthday and anniversary gifts for her travelers celebrating those occasions.

It was after 1:00 p.m. when she got back to the hotel and dropped off her packages. She was free until 5:00 p.m. when they would depart for the included show out on the strip. She changed into jeans and a T-shirt. She decided she would gamble a little and when she did she always went to the Plaza, a casino about one and half blocks from her hotel. She called the Plaza her "hideout" because she would never run into any of her passengers there and could have some time alone.

As she left the side door of the South Tower she could see the Plaza down the side street. She put on her sunglasses and a baseball hat that completed her outfit. As she crossed the road she saw the street ahead of her lined with motor coaches. As she neared the end of the block she saw a bus from Chase's company. She knew there was only a slim chance that he would be on the bus but she thought she would stop and say hello to the driver. She would ask him to tell Chase hello from her the next time he saw him.

She knocked on the bus and stood back waiting for the door to open. Because of her hat and sunglasses her face could not be seen. She was shocked when Chase appeared! He had been resting in one of the passenger seats and had to stand up to open the door.

Speechless at first she could not say anything. She watched him look at her from head to foot with those hooded eyes of his. She knew he did not know who she was. She took off her sunglasses and tucked them into her scooped-neck T-shirt. As she jumped on the coach she removed her baseball cap and said, "Do I get a hug?"

She heard him gasp when he realized who she was. She put her arms around him but just gave him a quick hug. She did not trust herself to do more than that and he was so shocked he did not hug her back.

"You look incredible."

She realized she was almost thirty pounds lighter than when he had last seen her. As he sat down in the driver's chair she sat in her favorite seat and put her feet up as she thanked him.

"I met a guy. He helped me feel good about myself again."

She started telling him about her group from Wisconsin and he replied that he would only be there for another hour when his tour would be leaving Vegas to return to Seattle.

She knew he did not like to talk about personal issues in their lives but she did tell him how, even though she was wearing pants three sizes smaller than she had worn in fifteen years, her husband had never noticed her weight loss. She also told him how she felt completely invisible to Ted. She saw him wince when she said that.

She did not bother going in to all Ted's physical problems. She really did not want him to know all her personal issues.

Next she told him about her friend Max dying. Since she had time and was trying to keep things on an impersonal level she also launched into her story of Dean, her Colorado driver. He just shook his head when he heard about the luggage and the dirty windows.

Finally she told him about the cruise and how much fun she had. He gave her one of his piercing looks when she told him how right he had been, but she knew it was best to ignore the way he was looking at her.

As usual she was monopolizing the conversation. One of the things she missed was how easy it was to talk to him about anything. She also remembered how he constantly made her laugh and now he was again throwing out his quick comments during her stories that made her laugh as usual.

Suddenly he asked her, "What does your friend think about you losing all that weight?"

At first she did not know what he was talking about and then she realized he meant "the guy" she had told him had made her feel good about herself again.

"He doesn't know. I never told him and I have not seen him in a while."

Asking her if she thought that was fair she just shrugged her shoulders.

It was happening again. The way he looked at her with his bedroom eyes was giving her a stomachache. There was a raw desire she felt just being around him. She wondered if she would always feel this way when she was in his presence.

She could not believe she had gotten this chance to see him again even if it was only briefly. She knew she liked him more than she should, but since nothing was said on the surface, she could ignore the obvious undercurrents that were going on between the two of them.

Deciding to get off the subject of "the guy" she had met she asked him about his girlfriend, Lila. He told her they had broken up right after Christmas.

"That must have been sad."

"It was."

"Are you going out with anyone else or have you retreated to your cave?"

He just laughed at her. As usual getting more than a few short sentences out of him was extremely difficult.

"If things work out I am planning on living somewhere on the Pacific Coast this next summer. I am planning on going to Portland or Seattle. My company has a lot of tours out in the Northwest this upcoming summer and I just need to be close to an airport for when I need to fly to some destination. It sure will be a lot better than flying four and a half hours one way from Wisconsin to get there."

He just listened as she continued.

At this point I am leaning towards the Seattle area

since the airport would probably be easier to fly in and out of. And then I can go exploring when I am not on tour. As long as national travel remains strong I could live on the Oregon coast the following summer."

"If you do get out by my neck of the woods I will look forward to seeing you and going for steamed clams."

She was hoping since she had the chance to tell him about her plans they would really happen for her.

Before she knew it time was up. Chase had to go pick up his travelers and head home. As she stood up to leave she reached up and gave him another quick hug good-bye. This time he hugged her back.

Although they did not press tightly together and he did not kiss her cheek as he had at the airport it felt good to be close and touching him again. She realized she had missed being around him more than she should. Once again she had that same sensation of "fitting" when she hugged him like she had at the San Francisco airport.

Not Ted or anyone else she had dated before getting married had ever given her that feeling. Since neither of them let their guard down when they were together she wondered if he felt anything for her. She could not believe he did not feel something with the way he looked at her even though no words passed between them.

As she was going out the door he caught her arm and said, "Nikki, tell that guy what he did for you. He deserves to know."

As he released her arm she jumped off the last few steps of the bus and onto the sidewalk. She put her baseball cap and sunglasses back on and turning to look back at him, she said, "Chase, I just did!"

She watched his eyes widen with understanding. With that she turned back towards the Golden Nugget and with a wave walked away as quickly as possible. She heard the bus start up and as she turned she watched him drive around the corner.

She could not believe she had told him. It seemed like she always lost control just before leaving him.

Chapter Twenty-Seven

Before she knew it her trip was over and she was back in Wisconsin with Ted. Meanwhile her brother Randy had friends who had moved to the Seattle area. He had mentioned to them about his sister wanting to live on a boat.

There was a man who worked in Everett at Boeing with Randy's friends who had a houseboat. He would be spending the summer working on the East Coast and was looking for someone who would watch over his place while he was gone. All she had to do was pay the five hundred dollars a month docking fees and the place would be hers.

Once again she could not believe things might work out for her move to Seattle. But how would she ever tell Ted? She knew she needed to spend the summer alone. She did not know if their marriage would last but she knew she needed time away from him.

Ted had already told her he did not want to leave Wisconsin and his doctors. As usual it was all about him and his wants and desires. Maybe things would be better between them if they separated. She knew at the present she was angry with him all the time and she did not think it was fair to either of them to live that way.

She checked with the lady who had watched over Ted when she went to Vegas. The woman was willing to come in for four to five hours a day Monday through Friday. She would charge two hundred dollars a week which Nikki thought was reasonable.

The woman was retired and alone and knew the extra money would come in handy. Besides there was not a lot she needed to do besides some grocery shopping, cooking and taking Ted to his doctors.

Nikki had a cleaning lady come in every two weeks and she planned to continue that service. She would take care of the big cleaning. With everything falling into place her only worry was agonizing over how to tell Ted.

After several days of apprehension she decided to speak to her sons. She knew they had to know what she was planning since they would be responsible for checking on their dad all summer.

Even though the housekeeper would actually take care of him they could take turns watching over him on weekends. Since Ted was happy with TV and reading his newspaper all day, there was not a whole lot anyone could do for him.

Actually her sons were much more supportive than she would have guessed.

"Mom, Brandon and I are really worried about you. We know how hard it has been for you taking care of dad in addition to working, and we do not want you to get sick too."

"Kyle, I cannot tell you how much it means to me that the two of you understand what I am going through. I need a break from this life with your dad. I keep thinking if I go away for the summer he will appreciate me more when I come back. I would call him every week to make sure everything is going well and I promise to come back at a minute's notice if there is any trouble. I do not want you boys to be saddled with the responsibility of all his medical problems."

"Don't worry, mom," Brandon spoke. We both know dad has never been a particularly happy person. Whether you are here or not will not change that. Between the two of us and the housekeeper we will watch over him and take care of any medical issues that arise. You will not need to come back. Just have a good summer and stay healthy."

"I don't think I should say anything this early to him or he might work himself into a tizzy. I have a trip in a couple of weeks to Washington DC for the cherry blossom festival. I will only be gone six days. I was thinking we could tell your dad when I get back.

That would give us a few weeks to get everything organized and for me to decide on a place to live for the summer. Although I have to tell you the houseboat Randy found in Seattle sounds really fun to me as well as reasonable."

Both boys nodded in agreement. Since their mother did not have any work scheduled in May they thought that would be plenty of time to get their dad used to the idea and get everything in place for the summer.

None of them had any idea that all this planning would be for naught. For the present she felt her heart lifted from the burden she was enduring. And her sons felt that in a small way they were helping their mother better cope with the situation she was living with.

There were no leaves on the trees this far north in early April. However the sun was shining brilliantly the day her bus left Chicago headed for DC and the cherry blossom festival. She could not help feeling good about the direction her life was about to take.

Chapter Twenty-Eight

The trip to DC was a fun trip Nikki really enjoyed. Although she had to admit she liked it better in May when the azaleas were in bloom. Cherry blossom time was beautiful but Nikki did not like all the crowds of people and absolute gridlock one usually encountered in the city at this time.

The passengers loved going to all the different monuments but usually at that time of the year there were so many people in the area it would take the coach one hour to get to someplace that would only take ten to fifteen minutes any other time of the year.

They arrived in the DC area Friday afternoon and stopped at Arlington National Cemetery before checking into their hotel for the next three nights. The next morning was the parade and Nikki wanted to arrive early. That was the only way the bus would find a decent place to park.

Her driver, Phil, headed for Madison Street. It was one block behind Constitution Avenue where the parade was held. The next street after Madison was Jefferson. Between these two streets was where the National Mall was located. It was not really a mall like a normal mall. Rather it was a large park that ran right through the center of downtown.

On one end was the Lincoln Memorial and reflecting

pool. Then the Washington Monument was situated in the middle of the Mall. After that was a large grass like area that led to the United States Capitol building. Two miles separated the Lincoln Memorial from the Capitol building. In the grassy area between the Capitol and Washington Monument were Madison and Jefferson streets with several of the Smithsonian Museums lined on either side.

She and her driver knew buses were allowed to park on Madison. They wanted the spot right between the National Museum of American History and the National Museum of Natural History. One building contained all the gem stones including the Hope Diamond and the other the First Ladies gowns. These were always the two most popular attractions. In addition to being right by the Smithsonian's two most requested museums they would only be one block from the parade route.

They arrived about an hour before the parade started and the Smithsonian buildings were not yet opened. Telling her travelers they needed to leave a little early everyone was on the coach right on time. It was important to get there early before anything was opened or they would never find a decent place to park the bus.

Within ten minutes of arriving they noticed all the bus spaces were filled. The travelers were happy they had come early. Now they were right in the heart of all the action and if they got tired it would be easy for them to come back and rest on the motorcoach while still being close to the parade and museums.

The only sight opened that time of the morning was the visitor center for the White House. It was about five blocks from where they were parked. All but a couple of her tour members walked over to the visitor center with her. They also stopped in front of the White House and took pictures since the public was no longer able to tour that building, except in special circumstances, due to increased security.

The day was busy and trying to see as many monuments as possible took up the whole afternoon and early evening.

The next morning they were on the road by 8:00 a.m. and off to see George and Martha's place—Mount Vernon—and a boat ride on the Potomac. The afternoon was opened for whatever they wanted to do.

Wanting to give their travelers more time at some of the other Smithsonian venues was part of their plan so they headed back to the city. This time there was no place to park except in a short term drop off spot on Madison Street.

Phil had to take the coach somewhere else in the city during the time they would be staying downtown. She told everyone their driver would be back in three hours and they should all meet at the same place he dropped them off. Then they would go to dinner.

Across the Mall to the National Air and Space Museum was the direction she was headed. It was a newer building and she had not had a chance to go through it yet. As she exited after touring that building she was thinking about going next door to the Native American Museum which had recently opened.

However as she looked up at the line of motorcoaches she could not believe her eyes. It could not be possible. Parked right in front of her was a motorcoach from Seattle. She could not imagine she would be lucky enough to run into Chase here.

Immediately, she went over to the door and knocked. Within a few seconds the door opened and her heart skipped a beat when she saw who the driver was.

"Oh, my gosh! Chase. Are you really here?"

"Nikki. I don't believe it. It just seems impossible we could actually run into each other like this in all these crowds."

"What are you doing here so far from home?"

"Actually, I am on a three week cross country trip. There are forty-five people on this journey. Since I have so much seniority and the tour manager recommended me, I was able to do the trip. We have worked together before and I like working with her. I was thinking about you when we were touring around Chicago. I knew you did not live too far from that city."

"We head back to Chicago tomorrow."

"We will be going to New York tomorrow. I hate trying to get around that city. It is another bus unfriendly city like San Francisco. Then when we finish touring New York we will head back to Seattle."

She realized she had not hugged Chase. She was so rattled seeing him so far from home. The chances of them running into each other seemed astronomical. But then again considering that over a million people attended the Cherry Festival maybe it was not so implausible after all. This was a big attraction for many tour companies.

Once again they only had an hour together and time seemed to fly by as they caught up on what trips they were doing. She decided not to mention her probable separation from Ted. She did tell him she was considering the possibility of renting a houseboat in Seattle for the summer. He just assumed her husband would be coming with her.

"Have you found a new girlfriend yet?"

"No, but I've been pretty busy. And maybe I still feel a little burned from my experiences with Lila."

"Would you tell me why you broke up with her?"

"It was pretty simple. Lila decided she wanted to

get married and I did not want to commit to her. We had issues that were unresolved and I felt marriage was the worst thing we could do. She accused me of being commitment phobic and maybe she's right. I probably am.

But at the same time it never felt right with her. We were like two people who liked being together because it was comfortable and we did not have to worry about finding a date for the weekend. That is definitely not a good reason to get married."

"You are right. Both of you would probably have been miserable after a few months and wondered how to reverse the mistake."

"I know I would have. But I do not think Lila would have. She wanted to get married and I guess she was at the point where she did not care who she married. We broke up right after Christmas and she was engaged to a friend of mine by Valentine's Day. They just got married two weeks ago."

"I am sorry, Chase.'

"Don't be. I would have been unhappy being married to Lila. I want to spend my life free."

Looking at him the ache was back in her stomach. As she glanced his way she wondered what it would be like if he kissed her. She knew she had to get past those thoughts. She was a married woman. However since she had not been kissed in over four years she realized that was probably causing the pent up desire she was feeling. However the biggest problem she was having at this particular moment was having a hard time not imagining his lips on hers.

He had never given any indication he thought of her in anyway except as a friend. As usual she could not read what he was thinking.

Before she knew it their time together was over.

She knew she had to get back to her travelers and Chase knew his passengers would be showing up at any second.

As she started leaving she heard him say, "Nikki, where's my hug?"

Turning back with a smile she put her arms around his neck to hug him. As she did she felt him put his arms around her waist and pull her close. She could feel his heart beating next to hers. Maybe just maybe he was feeling as much for her as she was for him.

Although she did not hug him as tight as she had at the San Francisco airport, she did press her body close to his. It was as if neither of them wanted to separate and the hug lasted longer than a casual one should have.

With their arms still entwined they broke apart and stared into each other's eyes. She had a feeling she was about to be kissed and her lips parted in anticipation.

All of a sudden she heard "Hi, who are you?" Chase's tour manager was back.

Quickly moving apart, he introduced her to the woman. Feeling very flustered she hastily said good-bye. She needed to get back to her bus and calm down a little before her travelers returned.

As she walked back to the coach she had tears in her eyes. She knew Chase affected her in ways he should not. The problem was she was powerless to change the feelings she was developing for him.

Meanwhile he was experiencing his own difficulties.

"Wow, Chase, do you have a girl in every port?"

Knowing in the past he had liked to brag about his conquests with women, his tour manager was shocked when he sat back in his seat with a scowl on his face and said nothing.

Chapter Twenty-Nine

Nikki had been back from DC for a week and she finally decided she and Ted would go out to dinner the next night so she could tell him about her summering in Seattle. Her sons had offered to be with her when she told him but she thought it was better if she did it herself. She also felt there was less likely to be a big scene if they were in a public place. However once again she discovered events were about to spin out of control.

The next morning as Ted was coming down the steps for breakfast he cried out in pain and fell on the last two steps. He had his hand on his back as he lay on the floor and he seemed to be in incredible pain. Nikki called for an ambulance to take him to the hospital.

The news was not good. His herniated disc was causing excruciating pain. The only option was to operate. The doctors were concerned with his poor health but there was no other way to relieve the suffering.

Calling her sons, they said they would get to the hospital as soon as possible. She told them the doctors would be starting the operation as soon as they sedated Ted.

She went in to see her husband before the operation. His pain was not as severe since he had been given a large dose of pain medication. She leaned down and kissed him on the cheek. She told him he would feel a lot better after the operation.

He smiled at her and gave a thumb's up sign as they wheeled him into the operating room. Then she returned to the waiting room where she knew her sons would look for her.

Her boys arrived at the hospital at the same time about an hour later. It was another half hour before the doctor came to find them.

The news was extremely grim. Ted had suffered another stroke while on the operating table. This had been a major concern of his doctors before the operation. He was in a coma.

The doctors felt he would eventually awaken but they told her, he would probably be in a "persistent vegetative state" for the rest of his life. This meant even though he appeared awake he would not be able to respond to anyone. The doctors also told her that coma patients could live like that for many years.

Nikki was devastated. The doctor said as soon as Ted was stabilized, which would probably be in a couple of days, it would be best for her to arrange to put him in a long term care facility that dealt with this type of brain injury. For all intensive purposes any normal life with him was over.

She and her sons talked about all their options but they knew they were pretty limited. She knew she was going to have to work more jobs to afford Ted's care. They had money set aside in case of illness but she knew the money would be depleted very rapidly if she did not try and keep adding to it.

A few days after moving Ted to the long term care facility she called her boss about more summer work. He told her he would be able to give her two tours a month starting in July. She hoped she would not burn out but she knew she needed the money. He told her they would be national trips out West. He assured her that the coaches were all full so he knew her tips would be good.

Talking to her sons about the summer they both agreed it was going to be very hard on her constantly flying such long distances, in addition to working so many days without a break.

Kyle told her he had some friends, a married couple, who were desperately looking for a place to rent. They were willing to pay eight hundred a month plus utilities. They were only in Wisconsin on a temporary basis so they were not interested in buying anything. Her condo would be perfect and was in a great location close to both of their jobs

Brandon reaffirmed that they thought she should go live on the houseboat in Seattle. Not only would she have enough money to pay the docking fees, but she would also have an extra three hundred dollars a month cash flow from the rental on her Wisconsin home. More importantly she would be much closer to her work living in Seattle and would not have to spend all those extra hours every month flying to and from her various destinations.

Both Brandon and Kyle knew their dad would never again be cognizant of any of them. While she was away both boys would take turns visiting their father and she would not have to worry about whether he was being properly taken care of.

The important thing now was that she earn some extra money to help with his costly upkeep. Since summer and fall were when the most jobs were available she needed to take advantage of that.

Knowing she would be away from her children until sometime in October she felt a little better when her sons reassured her. They knew it would be better for her to be out West closer to her wok instead of constantly commuting back and forth. Besides neither of them had seen that part of the country and they told her they would come visit her on the houseboat.

Although he was still alive, realistically she had to keep reminding herself that her life with Ted was essentially over. The boys both felt she needed some emotional happiness to help make her work less stressful and they knew she would love living on a houseboat for the summer.

Her boys felt the opportunity for the boat had come about for a reason and she was meant to take it. They also promised they would definitely come out in the summer to visit her when she was not working so she would not feel so lonely. Brandon was a baseball fanatic and thought he would plan his visit to Seattle when the Chicago White Sox, his favorite team, played the Mariners.

She smiled for the first time in days at Brandon's reference to the White Sox. Kyle picked up the phone and called his uncle. Randy was happy to make the call and line up the boat for her. Even he thought a trip to Seattle in the summer sounded like fun.

Now she realized that between tours she would have lots of visitors. She also knew she should not feel so happy considering her husband's condition, but she felt a lightness in her heart that had been missing for a long time.

The next two weeks sped by as she made sure all of Ted's arrangements were taken care of. She also had all her personal items stored so the renters could move into her condo. The only thing to put a damper on her spirits was Ted's condition. She knew he would hate living like he was but she was powerless to do more for him than provide for his costly care.

Not being able to keep from smiling she loaded the last few items into the car for her trip out to Seattle. The boys had been over the evening before to help her pack the car and take her out to dinner. She had arranged for a cleaning service to come into the house the next day and Kyle would meet the renters in the evening to turn over the keys to them.

Everything was taken care of and she experienced an indescribable feeling of joy as she left her driveway. She was determined to forget all the loneliness she had gone through the past few years. There was no way of knowing what might have happened if she had told Ted about the separation but now she could look forward to tomorrow with anticipation and perhaps some happiness. And she and her husband had not had to go through the agonies of a trial separation, although she would have preferred that to what he was going through now.

Chapter Thirty

As soon as she got settled into her houseboat she sent Chase a letter to his bus company since she did not have his address or phone number. She wrote that she was leaving June eighteenth for a seven-day trip to LA but would be back on June twenty fourth. She would have fifteen days free before her next trip to Montana and Glacier National Park.

She loved her life at the marina. Everyone living there was like family and she knew while she was away on tour she would not have to worry about her things. Everyone knew everyone else's business and she really did not mind. They were not being nosey. They were just protective of everyone who lived there.

It seemed the "boat people" always knew when to party and also when to step back and give each other space. Every Thursday night they would have a potluck dinner to welcome the weekend. There would be anywhere from ten to twenty people and they always had a lot of fun.

Before she knew it the eighteenth arrived and she flew to Los Angeles for her Hollywood tour. It was a unique one time trip her company had set up for a special group. The trip was wonderful and she especially liked going to Catalina Island. She had been there a couple of times before and always enjoyed visiting that area.

When she arrived home the message machine on her phone was flashing. As she suspected it was from Chase and the news was not good. He was on his way to Canada and had been assigned two back-to-back Canadian Rocky tours. He would not be back until the day she left for Montana. He knew they had a week after her tour before their Pacific Coast trip and told her he would call her when she got back from Montana.

She continued to have fun with her "boat" friends and as promised, Brandon came to visit for five days. He spent three of his five days at the ballpark, but since she was busy preparing for her Montana tour she was glad she did not have to entertain him very much.

Besides Brandon might come out for another visit that summer. He had met Brooke, a young widow who owned the boat next to Nikki's, and they had spent almost every evening together. Brooke enjoyed baseball as much as Brandon and went to the last two of his games with him. The only problem was she would root for the Mariners which created a little friendly tension between the two of them.

Nikki had totally given up on ever being a grandmother. She could not believe there might be some hope in that area yet if Brandon and Brooke got together. The only problem was the long distance relationship that was involved. Many times that became insurmountable for many developing relationships.

Brandon left the day before her tour and Brooke offered to drive him to the airport. Nikki smiled as she saw the twinkle in his eyes as he hugged her good-bye. He mentioned something about returning for a visit later in the summer and she told him to come anytime he wanted. Even if she was on a tour, her boat was always available for him. She noticed the two of them look at each other rather shyly when she mentioned that.

Before she knew it the next day had arrived and she was off once again on another adventure. Glacier Park was always a fun place to go especially when the jammers drove the red buses along the Going-To-The-Sun Road. This highway was named one of the top one hundred scenic roads in America and it did not take much to understand why.

She also enjoyed the day trip to Alberta, Canada and the boat ride they took on Waterton Lake. They saw some brown bears roaming the streets in Waterton. Even though that was a common sight in town, it always amazed her. In addition to the boat ride, before going back to their lodge at Glacier, they made a stop for high tea at the famous Prince of Wales hotel located on the lake. She wondered if she would ever get lucky enough to stay at the POW, as the locals referred to it.

As they were leaving Waterton her driver missed the turn and two UFE'S happened because of that. As they were driving down the wrong road a moose came barreling out of the forest. She realized they would never have seen the moose if they had taken the right turn. It was such an amazing sight and all the travelers clapped thinking the driver had ordered the moose to come out on the road at just that moment.

By the time they realized they were going the wrong way they were at the point of no return. Looking at the map it did not make any difference mileage-wise if they continued on taking the next major road south or go back the way they were supposed to. They decided to try the new route and ended up going through a town near the border that had a fountain dedicated to a native daughter—Fay Wray. She liked visiting new places and knew she would never see the words "King Kong" again without thinking about that little town.

This time her group came from the Midwest and Florida. They had a lot of fun together, but as much as she was enjoying the trip she could not keep her mind off of finally seeing Chase again. She was glad when the nine days were over since she could hardly wait to get back to Seattle.

Randy was coming for a visit and she was looking forward to playing tour guide with him. She also hoped she and Chase would get a chance to go out and have a drink some evening before their tour together.

She knew she should not even consider a possible relationship with him. A romance might happen but she was not interested in any long-term relationship. Besides she was definitely going back to Wisconsin in October when her tour season ended.

If nothing happened between them that would be okay, too. She just wanted to be friends with him. She enjoyed his company and felt she could talk to him about anything. She also wanted to tell him about her husband so he would have a chance to decide how serious or not he wanted to be in a possible relationship.

Once again her message light was blinking on her answering machine when she got home. And once again it was bad news from Chase. His mother had been rushed to the hospital and was probably going to need heart surgery. His message said he would let her know what was happening as soon as he knew something.

Having a momentary thought that the "gods were conspiring against them," she wondered if maybe the two of them were never going to see each other again.

Randy arrived the day after she came back from Montana and that helped to take her mind off of not seeing Chase. He was going to be with her for a week and was looking forward to touring as much of the area as was possible in that short time. Randy was also a fitness buff and loved hiking so some jaunts to the mountains would be essential.

And so when her brother arrived, Nikki, the tour guide went into action mode.

One day they spent going up to the Ross Lake National Recreation Area. They walked the Diablo Lake area and visited the historic Diablo dam which was the source of Seattle's electricity supply.

They were in the heart of the Cascade Mountains and the scenery was stunning. The lakes had the beautiful blue-green color that was caused from the glaciers. And in some areas they were completely encircled by mountains. It gave one the feeling of being totally alone in the world out in the middle of nowhere. Randy mentioned how amazing the mountains were with the different shapes that erosion had created and as they hiked they never got tired of looking at the scenery.

On another day they drove up to Mount Rainier National Park. She was really happy the mountain was out that day. So many times a cloud cover encircled the top of that volcano.

They stopped at the visitor center at Paradise and then had a nice lunch at the lodge. Then her brother insisted they climb up onto the glaciers that surrounded them. She smiled to herself as she was ascending the mountain realizing she was doing things she would never have conceived of just a couple of years previously.

As they were getting ready to leave Paradise she saw a bus from Chase's company. She knew he would not be there since the drivers bid for particular tours and would work at those jobs on the same days all summer long.

However, she went over and talked to the driver. She

told him she was Chase's friend as well as a tour manager. The driver mentioned his mother had heart surgery the day before and she told the driver that he had left her a message that might happen.

What she was really interested in knowing, since this was her first visit up to Mount Rainier, was if there was any place she and her brother should not miss seeing. The driver, eager to share his knowledge, told her about a pullout where he went with his passengers after lunch. It was not too far from Paradise on the way back down the mountain. There was quite a steep walk about a quarter of a mile down some steps to a beautiful waterfall, but well worth the hike.

Realizing this was just the type of place Randy would love the driver pointed out exactly how to get there on her park map. It was only a few minutes later that they found the pull-out and the two of them made their way down the steps.

The sun was shining brightly and when they got to the bottom they saw a spectacular rainbow. That had definitely been worth the hike down. As they climbed the steps back up to the parking lot she saw the bus drive in. She went over and thanked the driver and told him about the wonderful rainbow. He had a knowing smile as he nodded his head at her.

She could not believe how quickly the week with her brother sped by. He was leaving Friday morning and her tour from Seattle to San Francisco would begin on Saturday. On Thursday they spent the morning around downtown but that afternoon she decided to show Randy one more waterfall.

Snoqualmie Falls was about thirty miles from downtown going east on Interstate 90. It was a favorite place for the people of Seattle to hike or picnic. The falls measured two hundred and sixty eight feet from top to bottom and contained an underground power plant. There was also a famous hotel and spa at the top. Almost every tour group that came to Seattle for a convention was taken to Boeing Field in the morning and the falls in the afternoon.

As they drove by the hotel she saw that there was an upper parking lot that was built for all the tour bus parking. She and Randy headed for the lower parking lot that was closer to the falls. As they got out of the car she noticed two motor coaches from Chase's company in the upper parking lot. Since he did the longer trips, especially to the Canadian Rockies in the summer, she knew he would not be there.

As they walked down the path the falls came in view. They both stopped suddenly. The sight was incredible. There was a double rainbow right near the bottom of the falls. This was even more special than the falls up at Mount Rainier.

"I can see why you like it out here. The beauty in this region of the country is absolutely astounding."

"I could not agree with you more. We better get going. I want to miss rush hour and we need to get back to the boat so we can get ready for the party."

The two of them spent the evening on one of the other boats at the weekly potluck. They had just returned when she heard her cell phone ringing.

As she answered she heard Chase's voice and her stomach did its normal flip flop.

"Hi, Nikki."

"Oh, Chase, you sound so tired."

"I am. My mother had her surgery a couple of days ago and I have been practically living at the hospital. But it is amazing how much better she is doing in such a short time. Then at noon today I got a call from the office. One of the drivers got sick and they desperately needed me to fill in on his afternoon tour.

"That had to be hard for you."

"It was. But the doctor said my mother was out of the woods and should recover without any problems, so I decided to take the job. The man who got sick was a friend of mine and I wanted to help him out."

"So where did you go?"

"It was just a quick run out to Snoqualmie Falls."

"You're kidding. What time were you there?"

"It was about 3:00 p.m."

"I can't believe it. That's when my brother and I were there. Was that you parked in the upper parking lot? I saw two coaches up there. But I would never dream one of those buses would be you."

"That was me but why would you think I would be there. Normally I do the longer trips and you knew my mother was sick. I guess we just were not meant to see each other until our tour. It is amazing you have been here all this time and we have not been able to connect."

"I guess you are right. Will you be at the airport Saturday afternoon?"

She could not stop the tear that fell from her eye when she realized how close to Chase she had been that afternoon and never realized he was right there.

"That is why I am calling you. I am not planning on doing the Saturday airport pick up and I did not want you to count on me being there. I want to spend as much time as possible with my mother since we will be gone a week. As long as she continues to do as well as she has, I will definitely be at the hotel first thing Monday morning. Look for me about 7:00 a.m. with latte in hand."

Smiling at his last remark she hoped this time

things would work out for them. Monday would be July 26th and she had already been out in Seattle for close to two months. She wondered if she and Chase would ever be more than just friends.

She was also worried about telling him about her husband. She knew he did not like to talk about personal issues but she felt he needed to know about her current situation. He probably thought her husband was living on the houseboat with her.

"I will see you Monday morning then. Call me if anything new develops with your mother."

"I will. I am anxious to see you. We will have a lot of catching up when we finally get together again. It is hard to believe I have not seen you since April and DC."

"We can do a little catching up at lunch on Monday. Bye."

Breaking the connection she ached again at the thought of being so close to him that afternoon and not seeing him. Even his voice on the phone made her long to see him. She had the feeling Chase would be shocked to hear how life had changed for her when she finally saw him again. And she knew he would be doubly shocked if he had any clue how she was feeling towards him.

Chapter Thirty-One

When Monday arrived all her luggage was marked and sorted when Chase drove up. She could hardly wait to see him but knew she needed to act nonchalant. She, as well as Chase, would not want the passengers to get any hint of anything between them.

The two of them glanced at each other for a few moments longer than necessary and she thought of their previous meeting in DC. Then she gave him a very quick hug which he returned. He began to load the luggage as she prepared her coach supplies for their trip south.

When they arrived at their lunch stop at Coldwater Ridge, Chase mentioned he would like to share a sandwich with her. She was glad he wanted to but wondered how much food she would be able to choke down considering the ache was back in her stomach just being in his presence.

Since the day was fairly nice they took their lunch to one of the tables outside overlooking Mount St. Helens. Of course there were passengers everywhere, so they kept the conversation very light.

He told her about his mother's operation and recovery. He noticed she appeared distracted while he was talking which was not like her. Since he had not had much sleep in the last week he wanted to go back to the coach and rest a little.

"I need to talk to you before you go back to the coach."

"We don't want to get personal, Nikki."

"I know. But I do have something I need to tell you."

Thinking she was going to tell him about her brother's visit and/or new problems with her husband, he was shocked when Nikki recounted Ted's back trouble and operation and coma.

Then she told him how she ended up on the boat and mentioned how she was now working two tours each month to help with Ted's costly medical care. She valued Chase's friendship and wanted him to know her situation.

"I was going to separate from Ted for the summer. I guess it worked out well since I did not have to go through all of that. I still plan to return to Wisconsin when my tour schedule out here ends in October."

He seemed surprised by her statement that she had planned to separate from her husband, although now it was moot. He knew being married so many years, it was probably a decision she had struggled with.

She looked sad and he became upset.

"It is just not fair. You should not have to always be so alone. Your good nature and love of life should be shared by someone who appreciates you."

Looking at him, she smiled.

"Thanks. I feel better having told you."

The rest of the day went well and they were actually ahead of schedule by a few minutes when they entered Portland. Even though a few minutes did not seem like a big deal, it could mean a big delay if they ran into rush hour.

Once again their rooms were down the hall from each other. Giving her that funny smile he said he would knock on her door when he was ready to go to dinner.

As they entered the Italian restaurant, he once again led her to the empty stools at the end of the bar where they always sat. As usual their travelers took up every table in the bar since the special was only served in that area.

The two of them ordered the steam clams and decided to split a Caesar salad. She could not eat all her clams and Chase was happy to finish them for her. They talked about inconsequential things as their travelers kept coming up to ask questions while they ate. As soon as they finished their dinner they left the restaurant and headed back to the hotel.

Deciding she did not want to spend the evening in her hotel room she made up her mind to walk. Since exercise had become a way of life for her now and the heat of the day had past, she decided to walk in the riverfront park across the street from their lodging. As they neared the hotel she told Chase her plan.

"Do you want to walk with me or are you going to retreat to your cave?"

"I am really tired and want to go to my room."

"Then I will see you tomorrow morning."

She walked to the corner and started across the busy road to the park. As she crossed the street she felt him beside her.

Neither of them said anything. He had always kidded her about her non-stop talking while he had always been a listener. Finally he asked, "If we are both good listeners, who talks first?"

Shrugging, she was not sure what to say to him. She knew her friends would say that was a first for her.

They walked for two blocks. All of a sudden he took her hand in his.

"Is that a good idea?"

"Probably not."

She knew she was still legally married, even though

Ted was in a vegetative state from his operation. She wondered if she was being fair to Chase. However such a simple act like holding hands felt so good, she could not tell him to not do it. They continued walking for a few more blocks until they came to a park bench.

As they sat down he put his arm around her. Pressing closer to him she reached her hand up and entwined her fingers with the hand he had around her neck. Not realizing what she was doing, she rubbed the bottom part of his hand with her thumb. They sat there for several minutes looking at Mount Hood in the distance.

Finally he said, "Nikki, I have never known you to be this quiet."

"We are creating a UFE and I want to savor it."

"And, what is a UFE?"

"An unforgettable experience."

She put her head on his shoulder as she continued to rub his hand. They sat there another half hour without speaking. The ache never left her stomach but she knew she would always have the memory of the two of them together like this for the rest of her life.

She realized he had known many women and she felt he probably was not as affected by this experience as she was. As usual he was saying nothing and she was having a hard time reading him. Although he was a carefree soul he was also a very sensitive man.

When they got up to leave he held her hand once again on the walk back to the hotel. When they were two blocks from their lodging he released her hand. And knowing their passengers could be around they began to walk farther apart as they neared their hotel.

In the lobby he turned to her and said, "That was definitely better than my cave."

Looking at him she felt goose bumps on the back of her neck.

Chapter Thirty-Two

Sitting at a table eating breakfast, Chase sat down next to her with a plate of food from the buffet. Once again they would have the local step on guide so she had free time sitting in the back of the bus all day.

"What are you going to do today?"

Last year she had been studying the research for her next tour but her next trip would be a repeat of this one so she did not need to do any studying.

She knew that Chase was trying to keep the conversation light especially since there were passengers all around them in the dining room. She had a hard time looking at him. There was no denying the chemistry between them. She felt the air around them charged with electricity. She knew she had to get herself together. There were still six days of this tour and she needed to concentrate on her travelers.

"Chase, there is no denying something is developing between us. I am not sure where it is going or what you want from a relationship. I want you to know right now I cannot and will not commit to anything long term. I know I need to think things through and probably you do, too. When this trip is over we need to sit down and talk. Until then I want to keep things as casual as possible."

He nodded at her.

"I would still like to eat our meals together. I would miss you too much if we stopped doing that."

Looking at her, he said, "I would miss it too much, too."

Those words from him made her smile when she remembered how he used to always eat alone.

"It is too bad we did not meet sooner."

"We would not have been ready for each other. There were experiences that brought us to this point. I think our paths were destined to cross at this time in our lives but I don't know why."

He was just about to say something else when a passenger came up and sat down between them to ask some questions about the tour. After that, Becky, the local guide joined them at the table.

"I better get out to the bus."

Watching him walk away she knew she had to concentrate on Becky and her plan for the day.

That evening they once again went to the Italian restaurant.

"I swear you are going to turn into a clam the way you eat those things so often."

"Well if I do I wonder if clams and tuna fish get along together?"

This made her laugh and it turned out to be the icebreaker. All of a sudden they were back to their casual conversations. She knew they would have fun the rest of the tour and they could put their upcoming talk on hold.

The temperature had been extremely warm that day, even for Portland standards. They both agreed there would probably be a lot of passengers walking in the riverfront park that evening and they decided to go to their rooms. She had started reading a novel on the bus that day and she was anxious to return to her book. And, since Chase had been driving all day, he had all his paperwork to catch up on.

They continued along the coast and she was really happy the fog stayed away. Chase automatically stopped at her Oregon lighthouse even though she had not mentioned it.

There was something comfortable about being with a driver who knew what you wanted to do without having to say anything to him. They ran into a little traffic going into the city and she remembered how they had sailed through the last time.

She went to pick up her boat tickets for the next day and had a few calls to make to arrange for her airport shuttles. Up to this point in their relationship she had always paid her own way when they went out for a meal or a beer.

Walking down the hall after they had both finished their chores Chase turned and said, "I want to take you out for dinner tonight."

She knew he was in a good mood because he had been able to find a place to park the motorcoach right away. Every driver she met complained about the lack of bus parking in this city.

"I know where I would like to go. There is a little restaurant down on the wharf. Every time we drive by it on our city tour, Chris always mentions it. I am not sure what type of food it is but we really should try a place a local guide always talks about."

"I will pick you up in an hour."

Knowing she wanted to clean up and still had calls to make, he wanted to give her enough time. It ended up being close to 7:00 p.m. by the time they got to the restaurant. There would be a half hour wait for the table but Chase said they could go sit in the bar and have a beer.

As they were going into the bar they spotted Chris sitting with his significant other. They stopped at his table to say hello. When Chris knew they had a wait he asked them to join him and his friend. They had just been seated and had a table for four. They immediately said "yes."

The first thing Chris asked was if he would be seeing them at Starbucks for Chase's latte in the morning. Laughing she told the guide that Chase would definitely be there.

The restaurant was seafood and the meal was as good as Chris had promised. He sensed there was something different about their relationship but he never said anything. Instead he and his friend spent the next three hours telling them many stories of their lives growing up in this fun city.

The time passed quickly and she could not believe how late it was. She knew the two of them would be up at 6:00 a.m. Chase paid the bill and they both thanked Chris for letting them join him and his friend for such a nice evening.

As they walked back up the hill to their hotel Chase's hand brushed against hers and she shivered. She could not believe how such a slight touch could affect her so. Her first real date with Chase had been even better than she had imagined.

They had not been alone tonight but that was okay. They were being very careful since they were both working and their first commitment was to their travelers. They had a wonderful dinner with fun companions and they were feeling more comfortable with each other. Chase still did not let his guard down and was sometimes hard to read, but the more she got to know him the more she liked him.

The next morning's city tour with Chris went well, especially since the fog stayed away. Before she knew it the farewell dinner was over and everyone was being dropped back at the hotel. They were now at the point where the tour was essentially "over."

"Let's go for a beer. I'll knock on your door in about twenty minutes," Chase winked at her.

As they left the hotel she started turning the corner to the Sports bar.

"No, we are not going there." Instead he led her to a lounge about three more blocks away from the hotel. There was a band playing.

"Chris told me about this place. I thought you might like to go dancing."

She could not believe this was happening to her. She had been married close to thirty years but Ted had never once offered to take her dancing.

"I cannot believe someone did not snatch you up years ago, Chase."

"I have been with a lot of women as you probably can guess. I never really knew what I was looking for. But I am happy with my life the way it is."

"I know you are happy with your life. And I know you are 'commitment phobic', but that is okay. I am not looking for any long lasting promises."

Knowing they still needed to talk, she also realized if they were to have a good relationship, she needed to express her feelings and communicate with him. This would be hard for her to do and she suspected it would also be hard for Chase but it was the only way they would know what the other wanted.

The band was playing the Drifter's song, "Dance With Me." Putting both her arms around Chase's neck as they danced close together, he leaned down and kissed her cheek. Without thinking about what she was doing, she began to lightly kiss his neck. She slowly worked her way up to his chin. It seemed a natural gesture and it was not long before their lips met.

It was a magic kiss. Neither could stop as the kiss deepened. She felt all kinds of feelings assaulting her body. When they finally pulled apart, breathing hard, she looked at him and said, "Don't you know better than to kiss a woman like that who has not been kissed in over four years?"

Lowering his lips to hers once again, she lost all sense of time and place. She did not even care she was in the middle of a dance floor surrounded by people as her arms tightly encircled his neck and she pressed hard against him.

Chapter Thirty-Three

Nikki really thought long and hard about driving back to Seattle with Chase instead of flying. She knew it would be a great time to talk about where they were headed, as well as just spending some time alone together. However he had to overnight before getting home. She felt this might create an awkward situation. She wanted him to spend his time driving back thinking about what he wanted from this possible new relationship.

Nikki had definite views on the situation and was going to tell him. It was very exciting feeling the way she did about him but she had been through too much with Ted not to be cautious about a new romance.

If Chase did not like what she had to say, she felt it would be better to nip anything in the bud before it got to the point that one or both of them would be badly hurt. She did not want to lose his friendship if there was any way to avoid that; although maybe that way of thinking was naïve on her part.

She still woke up every morning with a feeling of freedom. As much as she thought of being in his arms and the pleasure that gave her, she was definitely not going to be tied down again.

Because of her decision, he dropped both her and the passengers at the airport. She was going to fly back to Seattle with the ticket her tour company had provided. This was Sunday and she would be home in a few hours.

Chase would get back and turn the motor coach in tomorrow evening. They agreed to meet for lunch on Tuesday. They would have ten days before their next tour together. He only had a couple of day trips scheduled during those ten days because he had not wanted to commit to too many long trips because of his mother's health. Due to his schedule they would now be able to spend some time together.

Being so busy with unpacking and reorganizing her tour materials and getting her reports finished and mailed to the office, Tuesday arrived quickly. Nikki saw Chase ride his Harley up to the gate of the marina right at noon.

He handed her a helmet when she went out to meet him for lunch. He asked her if it was alright to go to a restaurant he enjoyed that was north of the city along the coast. It was a beautiful day and the restaurant had a nice deck where they could sit outside and look at the water as they ate. He was hoping she would not mind the ride on his bike.

Nodding in agreement she climbed on the cycle. Her legs were pressed against his and she put her arms around his waist. She had never ridden on a motorcycle before but knew this would be an interesting experience. It was a good way to get close to him without his reading anything into her actions.

Crazy feelings she had long forgotten went through her body as her legs pressed against his. All too quickly they pulled up to the restaurant and were seated on the outside deck.

The waitress had just brought their drinks when her cell phone rang. It was a driver friend from Illinois. He wanted her to know that her friend Max had died the previous day. As she hung up the phone she had a hard time not crying. Knowing she had told him about Max when they met in Las Vegas last March he knew how sad the news made her.

"Do you remember on one of our first tours when you were talking about being a good listener?"

He nodded.

"For many months I use to call Max every weekend. He would tell me how his week had been and how he was eating and sleeping and what type of medicine he was being given; just day-to-day kinds of things. I would sit and listen to him and not say much of anything.

I would always think of you at that time and remember you telling me how sometimes we need to just listen. I think one of the reasons you came into my life was to teach me to be a better listener. I know it helped me be there for Max when he needed me."

Usually not at a loss for a quick comeback, he was not sure exactly what to say to her. Although the death had been inevitable it was still hard, especially when it was someone so young. Thinking about Max's death, made him reflect on his own life.

He knew he felt lonely at times. He had many relationships but he had never met anyone he wanted to live with forever. He liked his freedom and his home and his life. At least he thought that was what he liked.

Chase had never met anyone like Nikki before. Sometimes it bothered him that she seemed to know what he was thinking. And besides that she was on his mind constantly. He knew she had no idea how he was feeling about her, thinking he just wanted a fling.

He would not mind a long term relationship with her, just nothing permanent. She was correct in her assessment of him not wanting to commit to anyone.

Actually a casual affair with her was exactly what he was wishing for. He hoped that was what she also wanted.

However he respected her enough that he did not want to hurt her. She had so many heartaches in the past and he wanted her to have a happy life now. Their lunch was definitely not going in the happy nonchalant way he had anticipated.

"Where do you see our relationship headed, Nikki?"

"I have thought about it Chase."

Previously she would have responded with "whatever you want." But she was no longer willing to take a back seat in a relationship. They had to be equal and be able to talk to each other without the other person feeling slighted. She also was not willing to commit to any kind of long term relationship. She was interested in a sexual relationship with him if he was.

But she was definitely going back to Wisconsin at the end of October when her jobs out West were over. She was still married and was not sure how she was going to deal with that part of her life. She could not just walk away from Ted and her responsibilities.

Taking off her sunglasses she looked at him and said, "I want no strings and no commitments. However if I am going to have a sexual relationship, it has to be with someone I know and like. It has been over four years since Ted and I have been intimate and I am ready to experience and enjoy that part of life again. I am open to learning new things."

Leaning towards him as she continued, she placed her hand on top of his.

"From everything I have read, it is not possible to have a good relationship, whether sexual or not, unless the two people communicate. I cannot read your mind and you cannot read mine. We will have such a short time together.

We have to tell each other what makes us happy, sad, glad or whatever. I need to know what you like or don't like and I need you to know the same about me. I know I cannot tell someone those kinds of things unless I am with a person I trust and feel comfortable with. You can walk away at any time and so can I. I know neither of us will be clingy. I also need to know you have been tested."

Giving a sigh of relief, she finished talking. That was probably the longest most uncomfortable speech she had ever given. She wasn't sure whether to be embarrassed or just glad that she had been upfront with him and it was over.

To her surprise, he looked at her and said, "Nikki, you want exactly what I want."

Looking at him with a smile, she said, "steamed clams?"

Chapter Thirty-Four

Taking her back to the marina after lunch they sat together on the deck of her boat. Later as they watched the sunset, she marveled at the beauty in nature if one would just stop to enjoy it. They did not say anything to each other. But it was comfortable just sitting there holding hands and watching the colors spread across the sky as the sun disappeared on the horizon.

"I am a little embarrassed by what we are about to do. I have never been with anyone other than Ted and it has been well over four years."

"We will have fun exploring together."

She could not believe how exciting and at the same time scary that prospect sounded.

"I have a friend who has a place on Orcas Islands. He said I could use it any time during the week. I have never taken him up on the offer but I can call him and see if we could spend the next three days there. I do not have any jobs until next week and it would be fun to go somewhere different. I guess taking so many days off due to my mother's surgery is finally working to our advantage. And since she is doing so well and recuperating at my sister's house, now is a good time for me to get away."

She thought that sounded like a great idea. It was probably better for them not to be around the marina when they were together for the first time. She loved living there but she also knew her friends liked to drop in any time of the day or night when she was home. She knew she wanted to be alone with him in the beginning.

Telling her to be ready about noon the next day he planned to call her in the morning to give her any information she might need to know before leaving.

He could have sat there with her all night, but knew if he did not leave soon he would not want to leave at all. When he stood up to depart, he reached for her and pulled her into his arms. Once again she seemed to melt against him as he kissed her.

Her lips were so soft he felt as if he could kiss her forever. As she kissed him back she had an instant thought that even though she would be leaving him in a couple of months, she would never forget his kisses.

The next morning he called her with the news that his friend would not be able to go to his cabin on the upcoming weekend. So if they wanted to they were welcomed to stay through Sunday.

"That will give us five days, Nikki. And my sister has my cell number in case anything would come up with my mother."

"I will let my friends here at the marina know I will be gone until Sunday night. I know you said there were a couple of restaurants close to the cabin but I think I will also go to the store and get some beer and a few groceries for us."

Once again the time seemed to fly and before she knew it he was there to pick her up. This time he brought his car since they had suitcases and he planned to leave his car at the ferry parking lot.

It was now time for Nikki and Chase's next journey to begin. And although she felt a little trepidation, she was also excited about the experiences the two of them were about to share.

Chapter Thirty-Five

Taking the ferry over to Orcas Island had been a fun way to start their adventure. His friend had a small cabin that sat on a slight hill near the water's edge away from most civilization. Orcas Island, the largest of the San Juan Islands, was home to over 2,400 foot Mount Constitution. This was the highest point in that chain of islands.

From the mainland the volcanic peak, Mount Baker, part of the Cascade Mountain Chain, cast a shadow over the island. With the one mountain overshadowing the other, the island looked a little like the "King Kong" Island as they came in on the ferry.

There were a couple of little restaurants and a tiny grocery store about a mile from the cabin. They had purposely brought suitcases with rollers since they would not have a vehicle on the island. She had even put the beer and groceries in a suitcase so it would be easier to transport everything to the cabin.

As they walked up the sidewalk to the house they noticed a screened in porch that overlooked the water. There was a futon and a table and chairs on the porch. Obviously it was used for extra company. There was also a swing attached by chains to the ceiling.

The inside of the cabin was all knotty pine and there was a nice sized living room with a large stone fireplace that dominated the room. There was an overstuffed couch that faced the fireplace as well as other furniture scattered about. Besides a dining room table there was a breakfast bar that separated the kitchen from the dining/living room area.

Down the hallway there were two large sized bedrooms. One bedroom had a double bed and a set of bunk beds. This bedroom was obviously used for company. The bigger bedroom had a king sized bed. As they made up the bed they discovered it was a waveless waterbed.

Between the two bedrooms was a bathroom. She could not believe the bathtub. It was obviously a bathtub/hot tub combination. She could picture herself soaking in the tub surrounded by bubbles.

The cabin was incredible! She felt she could have moved into this house forever. It was the type of place you could come to and lock out the rest of the world. She was glad Chase had picked such a perfect spot.

She was still feeling a little uncomfortable with the situation she was in. As he brought some wood in from the porch and put it by the fireplace she found some empty drawers to put her clothes in. Deciding she had to let things take place as they would she came out of the bedroom just as Chase was bringing one last load of firewood in. He mentioned going for a walk after he had unpacked and she thought that sounded perfect. She decided to put the groceries away while he was busy in the bedroom.

As she was organizing the food in the cupboards he came up behind her. He leaned down and began kissing the right side of her neck. As she bent her head to the left he continued kissing her neck. Suddenly an onslaught of feelings tore through her body. As she turned towards him a can of tuna fish dropped from her hand and rolled on the floor. Neither of them was aware of the can dropping as she moved against him.

All she could think about was kissing him. She locked her arms around his neck, squeezing as she pressed against him. She could feel him against her. All thoughts of a walk totally left her as she moaned and pressed even closer.

The two of them never made it past the living room couch. Their clothes made a trail from the kitchen to the couch. She had forgotten how good it was to be with someone again. And Chase did things to her that she had never experienced before.

When it was over she was too weak to even move off the couch. She had been swept off her feet by his mind-blowing skill. She lay in his arms and marveled at how lucky she had been to find someone like him as a lover. She knew he would fill her life with pleasure as long as they were together. Sadly she realized that even though this would be a short-termed commitment he would always be in her heart.

Since neither of them had slept well the night before thinking about what was about to happen they fell asleep on the couch. It was almost two hours later when they began to awaken a little stiff from sleeping entwined together in such a small space.

As he was looking around the room for his jeans, he suggested it might be a good time for a walk. Even though it was summer, the wind was blowing and the coldness of the water surrounding the island kept the temperature a little on the cool side.

Putting on their jackets they walked hand in hand along the shore of the beach. Neither of them said anything to each other but the silence felt comfortable. They had no idea they were both thinking about how much fun it would be to shut out the rest of the world and spend weeks living like this together.

When they returned from their walk she was ready for a long soak in the hot tub. Even though she now exercised with her new lifestyle she had a feeling there would be parts of her body that would definitely feel sore by the next day.

As she lay in the tub with the jets swirling the hot water around her Chase came into the bathroom. He had two beer mugs in his hands. She noticed the slice of lemon in each mug. She also noticed his absence of clothes. Looking at him the ache in her stomach returned almost immediately. She could not believe she wanted him again!

As he lowered himself into the tub she leaned over and began kissing his neck and face until their lips once again met. As he pulled her on top of him she wondered how people could say love was only for the young.

When they finally got out of the hot tub they knew they needed to eat something; if for no other reason then to keep up their strength. Since the temperature was beginning to drop Chase started a fire in the fireplace. Putting on his long sleeve jean shirt she went to the kitchen and began making a cheese and veggie omelet for their dinner.

It was not long before she noticed him next to her wearing his typical off duty clothes—jeans and a white undershirt—beginning to make a salad. It still amazed her that he would automatically work in the kitchen, and knew exactly what to do without her asking him for help.

The two of them continued fixing their meal saying very little to each other. Working alongside him seemed so natural and comfortable she felt like they had been together for years rather than just getting to know each other.

She kept glancing at him as he was preparing the salad. She found it incredible after the day they had just spent together that she was still having a hard time keeping her eyes off of him.

After dinner they moved to the porch and sat on the swing and watched the sunset while holding hands. As the waves lapped against the shore she thought there could not possibly be a better way to spend a day. She realized that this was not reality but for a few days they could keep reality away.

When they finally retired they lay wrapped in each other's arms all through the night.

The next morning was spent walking along the shore. She marveled at the sea foam she saw along the beach. The sun was shining and rainbow colors could be seen in the foam. The wind was blowing slightly and as she glanced down the foam looked as if it were shivering. She thought to herself that was how she felt every time Chase looked at her.

There was a lot of driftwood scattered on the beach and they gathered up quite a few pieces so they would have a good supply of firewood. Then they walked to the nearest restaurant and had lunch. After having a bowl of chowder and splitting a grilled ling cod sandwich they stopped at the little grocery store for a few needed supplies before returning to their cabin.

Each day blended into the next and sped by all too quickly. They walked on the beach every morning. Then they would walk to one of the little restaurants for lunch. They made love every afternoon when they got back from lunch. After a nap they would spend hours sitting in front of the fireplace or on the porch swing, depending on the weather, getting to know each other better. Some nights were spent in the hot tub and others the waterbed. They were both getting much more proficient at knowing what each other wanted and needed.

One day as they walked to the little downtown area she spotted a boat leaving the marina. Since she was living on a houseboat she was not able to cruise the islands which she told Chase she would like to do.

"Yes, Nikki. Cruise here in the summer and the Caribbean in the winter. That would be your definition of a perfect life!"

She nodded in surprise that he remembered her dream.

Although he did not recognize the boat owner, Chase knew the man seemed familiar to him. Looking at the back of the boat as it left the dock Nikki noticed the name, "Journey Ahead." She thought that seemed an appropriate name for a boat.

All too soon it was Sunday. She knew that packing and leaving this place was going to be the hardest thing she ever did in her life. She was so thankful they had these few days alone together. She knew if he left her tomorrow he would be a part of her heart forever.

Some people never got so lucky. Thinking back she remembered the previous Sunday and how he had dropped her at the San Francisco airport. They had journeyed a long ways together in just one week.

It was hard to believe something this wonderful had happened to her. Ted's selfishness seemed a distant memory. She felt a quick stab of guilt thinking of how her husband's life had changed and how happy she was at this moment in time.

It was impossible not to agree with the saying: "life was not measured by the breaths one took but rather the moments that took your breath away." This had truly been one of those moments in her life.

Chapter Thirty-Six

Chase ended up working Monday through Wednesday but they were day jobs. He still had not scheduled any longer trips because of his mother's health issues. Since he lived south of Seattle and she lived north of the city, they needed to do some juggling to be together.

Monday night they spent at his condo and he made dinner. The next night was on her houseboat and she made dinner. Her friends at the marina knew something was happening in her life, especially since she had never had anyone stay over except family members. They were friendly when they saw her but no one dropped in unexpectedly when he was there.

On Wednesday evening he was finished with work until their next tour together. They would have an airport run on Saturday. He had already decided he would work on Sunday with her for the city tour rather than his company sending a relief driver. He wanted to spend the day with her and it would also give him a chance to get to know the travelers a little sooner.

Wednesday night they went to his favorite restaurant near his home. It was called Joseph's and was a combination Italian and seafood eatery. Naturally he planned to have his steamed clams. They sat up at the bar and had dinner. The restaurant was on the waterfront and the bar had large picture windows that overlooked a marina.

Chase introduced the owner of the restaurant to her. It was not a surprise that his name was the same as the restaurant. Joe was a short man, probably about five feet six. He was bald and had the greenest eyes she had ever seen.

Joe told her, even though he was Italian, there must have been some Irish blood in his family. When he had hair it had been more red than brown. He looked like he was in his early sixties. The thing that struck her was the sadness she saw in his eyes. He was constantly smiling at his customers but there was an overall sorrow to his demeanor.

Since Chase had been coming into his restaurant for several years, Joe knew him very well. He asked him where he was headed next. He told Joe about their upcoming tour down the coast. Thinking it sounded like fun Joe wished them a happy journey.

As he left them, he leaned over to her and said, "Take good care of him. He is a very special man."

As she nodded at Joe, he winked at her.

"Chase, what is wrong with him," she asked after Joe had moved to talk to some other people? "He looks like he just lost his best friend."

Sometimes he forgot how perceptive Nikki could be of other people she encountered.

"His wife, Theresa, died a few months ago. They were married when Joe was eighteen and they celebrated their forty-seventh anniversary just before she died."

"Wow, he has to be devastated."

"Everyone said it broke his heart. It's hard to believe a person loving someone else that deeply."

She gave him a funny look. "I am sorry it never happened for you."

"I am happier this way."

He might think he was happy but to her, he had seemed like a very lonely man from the very first moment she had met him. She hoped their affair was giving him pleasure. She knew he was giving her way more than she had ever expected. He was helping her let go of her past heartaches with Ted and the future looked brighter as her past was being forgotten.

She had recently been listening to a song that went, "if you smile every day, happy times are here to stay." She had always tried to smile at people even when she was having a down day. She now thought how he made her feel. She felt as if her heart was also smiling. She knew she had to be careful before she lost all her objectivity.

They spent Thursday night back at the marina. Needing to get packed up for her tour she wanted to get the place locked down since she would be away several days.

Chase had another day job on Friday. After so many days off he was looking forward to the work. Brooke needed to go to a meeting downtown that afternoon so she offered to drop Nikki off at her hotel.

She quickly agreed since that would give her a chance to question the woman about her son. Having been so tied up with Chase, she did not want Brooke to think she was ignoring her. She was looking forward to driving into town with the woman and catching up on all the news.

On their way to the hotel Brooke mentioned that she had been emailing back and forth to Brandon every day and she thought he might come out for another Seattle visit soon. Smiling Nikki wondered if perhaps something might develop between the two of them even considering how far apart they lived from each other.

Since she was required to be in place the day before the tour started and the room was already paid for by her company, Chase decided to spend the night with her. They would take advantage of the hotel facilities but he would go back to his condo when the tour actually started. They both thought it would be inappropriate for him to stay over when she was working.

When he arrived after work he suggested they walk to a little restaurant around the corner for dinner and drinks. She thought that sounded like a good idea. Usually she liked to have input into decision making but this was his town and she was glad he was teaching her about some of his favorite haunts. She was learning about places the average tourist would never find.

Rearranging some of her clothes to make room for his things she turned to ask him about going to the hot tub before dinner. All of a sudden being in a hotel room with him almost seemed like something forbidden.

Feeling herself getting weak as their eyes met she could not believe after ten days she could still be so affected by him when he looked at her. As he came towards her, she felt an unbearable ache for him and the last thing she said as her arms encircled his neck was "there goes dinner."

She was right! There was no dinner and no hot tub. By the time they got out of bed and took a shower it was time to sleep. They knew they would have to keep themselves under control during their tour and both of them had wanted to take advantage of their evening alone.

Tomorrow would be the first night they were not spending together since their affair had started. Realizing missing him in bed with her would keep her from sleeping well, she also knew it would be good practice. She had already told him she was not going to be sneaking down any hotel hallways while on tour and she would not let him either.

So much for using the hotel amenities she thought

as she lay wrapped in his arms just before falling asleep. Tomorrow they would be headed south on one more journey together and although they were working at least they would be with each other.

Chapter Thirty-Seven

After the airport run she stayed in the lobby until 6:00 p.m. answering questions and suggesting dinner options for her passengers.

Chase pulled up to the front door of the hotel at 6:30 p.m. and they went to dinner several blocks away. They sat close to each other and held hands throughout their meal.

She was not very hungry and he did not eat very much either. They just wanted to be close to each other but needed to stay far enough away from the hotel so their travelers would not run into them. They returned to the hotel about 9:00 p.m. and as she got out of his car she turned and saw the longing in his eyes.

"I am going to miss sleeping with you tonight."

"I am, too."

She kissed him quickly on the cheek. She did not want any passengers to see her with him but more importantly she did not trust herself to kiss him on the lips. She had a feeling she would not get out of the car if she did.

As suspected, she tossed and turned all night. She missed sleeping in his arms. She hoped he was having as much trouble as she was. The next morning when he pulled the motor coach up for the city tour she took one look at him and knew instantly that he also had a rough night.

She sat in the back of the coach as the local guide showed them the sites. Normally she enjoyed this city tour but today all she could envision was the things Chase had done to her in the last few days. She also imagined all the different things she wanted to do to him when she got her hands on him again. Whenever they got off the bus to see particular sights she had all she could do not to touch him.

The city tour finally ended at the Market. They dropped most of the passengers there and then they took the guide and the remaining travelers back to the hotel. The guide asked to speak to her.

Chase told her he had to leave and would be back in two hours to pick her up so they could retrieve the travelers from the Market area. He seemed very stiff and curt with her and she wondered if this was just his reaction to trying to keep his cool around her. She still worried that the man who liked to completely withdraw from time to time might return.

She spent ten minutes with her step-on. As soon as the guide departed she immediately went out of the hotel and walking to the corner turned left for her walk down the hill. She knew where the bus "hideout" was when the drivers had to wait in the city. As soon as she turned the corner from the hotel she saw the familiar colors of the motor- coach parked two blocks away. When she reached the bus, just as she had in Vegas and DC, she knocked on the door. It opened almost immediately. Looking in her direction he was sitting in the driver's seat with his logbook braced on the steering wheel.

Climbing up the inside stairs of the bus she said, "Lock the door. We only have two hours."

As the door closed behind her she grabbed his hand and led him towards the back of the bus. She was headed to the seats that were roomier for handicapped people. She reclined the back of the seat and had him sit down. She hungrily descended on his lips as she straddled him. She heard him moan and knew instantly she was where she needed to be. She did not know how she would spend another night without falling asleep in his arms but at least this time together would help both of them to better cope.

The next day went well. They had lunch together at Coldwater Ridge but went to a table outside so they could keep their sunglasses on while they ate. They were afraid the travelers might see the desire in their eyes.

In Portland as she finished up her duties on the coach she asked him what time they would go for dinner. To her surprise he told her he was not very hungry and planned on staying in his room that night. She had a momentary thought that the "old" Chase was back. She said goodnight to him and went up to her room wondering why his mood had changed.

It took her fifteen minutes to get unpacked and arrange all her paperwork on the table in the room. She was in the bathroom when she heard a knock on the door. She thought the knocking was strange since she had not given her room number to any of the passengers. She opened the door but there was no one in the hallway. As she closed the door she was thinking to herself that maybe she was losing it when she heard more knocking. She turned and realized the noise was coming from the connecting door in her room.

She opened that door and there was Chase with beers and a box of crackers in his hands.

"How did you get a room next to mine?"

"I know you said no sneaking down hallways. I have been coming to this hotel for years and know the manager quite well. Since we will be here two nights I asked her for the favor. I have never asked her for anything like that before so she was happy to oblige. I know we will not be able to do anything at our next two stops but I could not stay away from you if there was a way we could be together in a discreet way."

"What about your steamed clams?"

"I can always have clams."

The two nights in Portland were just what they needed to make it to San Francisco. They even went out for his steamed clams the second night. Now they both concentrated on their travelers.

Not wanting anyone to know there was anything going on between them, they were very careful what they said to each other. And they made sure they never got close enough to accidentally touch each other.

After arriving in San Francisco since they were in a big hotel in the wharf area this time she asked the manager for connecting rooms. The hotel was situated like a square inside and the staff always put the tour manager and drivers on a different floor from their passengers. She knew no one would know anything was going on. That is the way they both wanted it.

She was beginning to wonder what they would do when they went on separate trips. She was worried she was becoming addicted to him. Then the connecting door opened and as she looked into his eyes her only thoughts were of what would happen next.

Their last night in San Francisco, he once again took her dancing. They went back to the lounge Chris had told them about. She could not help thinking about how far they had come in just a few weeks.

Unlike their last tour this time she was riding back on the bus with him. They both wanted to spend as much time as possible with each other. There were only a few days before their next trips and this was the last one they were doing together. After their next tours September would be upon them and they would be into the busiest time of the year for touring for both of them.

Sunday dawned and later that morning she watched as the last of her travelers went through security at the airport. Then she went back outside the terminal to wait for Chase to pull around. It was not long before she saw the familiar bus. As he pulled up she quickly jumped on so he could keep going and avoid a ticket.

Normally he turned the bus in about 5:00 p.m. on Monday evening. Since they ended up spending a little more time in the overnight hotel than they had anticipated, it was 9:00 p.m. before he got the coach back to the "barn."

There were only six days before they were both going out again and this time it would be separately. He asked her if she wanted to do anything special in the short time they had left.

She wanted to go back to Orcas Island and the cabin but when he called his friend, he learned it was not available.

"Maybe we will be able to go back another time this fall."

Chapter Thirty-Eight

All she wanted was to be with Chase but she knew she needed to get ready for her next tour. Besides, the two of them both needed to take care of things at their homes. Chase wanted to take her to dinner at Joseph's again but she told him she would not be able to get there until after 7:00 p.m.

Instead it was almost 8:00 p.m. by the time she pulled up at his condo. There had been an accident on the freeway and she had been stuck for almost forty-five minutes.

"I am surprised you did not go get your clams without me."

Looking upset he said, "I was worried about you."

"I am sorry you were worried. I was already on the freeway when I realized I forgot my cell phone. By the time I got stuck in traffic there was not much I could do."

Since she was ready to go he got in her car for the drive to the restaurant. He had never ridden with her before and she was thinking how strange it was to be driving a driver. This was a first for her.

Since he seemed a little more quiet than usual she did not say anything either. She kept thinking how the next five days would probably fly by. After dinner she asked him if he wanted to walk down to the marina. They were holding hands as they strolled to the dock. For some reason one of the gates onto a pier was not locked and she asked him if he would mind looking at the boats with her.

As they walked on the dock she suddenly stopped. "Look. There is that boat, 'Journey Ahead', that we saw when we were staying on Orcas Island."

Glancing at where she was pointing he agreed that was definitely the same boat.

Just then the owner came out on the deck from inside the boat. It was Joe!

"No wonder he looked familiar to me that day."

Joe looked up and seeing the two of them waved at them to come aboard.

After they climbed on the boat she told Joe about seeing him at Orcas Island when they had been staying there. He responded by telling her how he and his wife, Theresa, used to go to the island frequently when they were out boating.

Chase jokingly told Joe about Nikki's dream to cruise the Caribbean in the winter. Joe told her he thought that definitely sounded like a lot of fun, and he hoped someday it would happen.

Then strangely the man said, "I see things have changed between the two of you."

Chase staring at Joe said, "What do you mean?"

"I can tell you two are closer to each other than before."

They looked at each other. They were not even holding hands and they had no clue how he could guess what was happening between them. They both tried not to show too much emotion in public. They did not want to accidentally slip if they were on a tour together.

"You have a way of looking at each other, as if you are secretly communicating, that was not there before.

Theresa would look at me the same way Nikki looks at you, Chase."

She shivered when Joe said that and she noticed Chase giving the man a funny look.

"What are you two planning for this week?"

They told him they really did not have any plans. They only had five days before they both were leaving on separate tours. Tomorrow they were spending the day at Chase's getting ready for their trips.

"We wanted to go back to Orcas but the cottage was taken already."

"Do you want to go out with me on the boat the day after that?"

"Oh, yes," she replied quickly.

Then she looked at Chase. She was thinking that possibly he did not want to spend the day on the boat.

Without her asking he replied, "Nikki, I don't care where we go as long as I am with you."

Joe had the feeling they had forgotten he was even there. He wondered if they realized that Chase had just read her mind.

The two of them thanked him, and told him they would meet him at 7:00 a.m. the day after tomorrow here on the dock. She mentioned packing a lunch but Joe told her no. He knew she was busy getting ready for her tour, and the restaurant always packed food and drinks for him when he was going out for the day. He told them he would tell the restaurant to pack enough supplies for three.

As she was driving back to the condo she asked him if he was sure he wanted to go out with Joe.

"I have been on many cruises. I like boats, too. I am just not as obsessed with them as you are. But I can see how boating could get in your blood."

When she stopped the car in his driveway she

leaned over and hugged him. She was so touched by his thoughtfulness she felt a tear run down her cheek.

Their lovemaking seemed to have an extra dimension to it that night. It was if Joe's words to them had pervaded their subconscious.

The next day they never left his condo. Chase was busy cleaning his place and she was finishing up her pre-tour paperwork. From time to time he would come and demand some of her attention.

She did not mind. In fact she could not believe how hard it was to keep her hands off of him. She did not know how she would stand being away from him for eleven days. She knew she had to get used to it. November would be here before she knew it.

That evening she again made omelets for dinner while he made a salad. As they worked together in the kitchen she was reminded of the happy memories they had shared on their first evening on Orcas Island.

Chapter Thirty-Nine

Walking onto the dock at exactly 7:00 a.m. they noticed the gate had been left opened for them. Joe had already stowed their food away and was just waiting for their arrival.

"You never showed us the inside of your boat."

Naturally he was thrilled to show them around. He had some special features built into the boat that he was proud to show off. The main cabin looked like any normal ship with chairs and a built in table. There were also benches that would convert into beds.

She also noticed how it was decorated and loved the blue and green color scheme that was scattered throughout the inside of the boat. The colors were a definite reminder of the sea.

The cabin cruiser was forty-five feet long so it was a good size. There was a small bedroom in the bow with two single bunks against each side of the boat. It was the aft bedroom that was a surprise. There was a queen size bed and it was her favorite, a waveless waterbed.

A small hot tub had been placed on the top deck. What fun it would be to sit in that tub at night and watch the stars. She realized the boat could not be more perfect.

As they re-entered the main cabin she said to Joe, "this is such a happy boat!"

At her words he turned white as a ghost. They both thought he might be getting sick. She quickly poured a glass of water for him but he was starting to get his color back and refused the drink.

"Theresa always used to say what a happy boat we had. When you used her exact terminology it surprised me. It was almost as if my wife was speaking to me again. It just took me unaware."

Feeling a little uncomfortable by his statement she asked, "How did you name the boat?"

Once again he told her it was his wife's idea. "Theresa always thought we had more journeys ahead of us.

"Personally I do not think you could have a more perfect name."

She had recently learned that Joe and Theresa had lost their only son during the Vietnam War. She realized that had obviously drawn them even closer together rather than apart as it did for some couples. As she sat down next to him, she put her arm around him saying, "thank you for taking us out with you today."

Chase had noticed before how Nikki had a way of comforting people when they felt sad. For the first time as he looked at her, his heart began to ache at the thought of her leaving in November.

It was not long before the boat left the dock. Joe asked if she wanted to take the controls. She once had an eighteen-foot ski boat but she had never piloted a boat this big. Then he told her since she planned to have her own boat some day it was about time she learned. He told them if they wanted to come out with him the next day he would let Chase pilot the boat.

She looked at Chase. Without looking at her, he said, "we would love to come out with you tomorrow. It will be fun driving something big besides a bus."

She and Joe both looked at him and laughed.

They cruised all morning among the islands that were scattered in Puget Sound. There were eagles flying close to the shore of several of the places they passed.

As she piloted the boat Joe pointed out markers and areas she needed to be careful around. He also showed her how to operate the different controls, and how to read the different settings on the control panel as well as the depth gauge.

Chase had gone to sit out on the aft deck. He had his swimsuit on and had taken his shirt off so he could get some sun. She had a hard time not constantly glancing at him. Joe watched with a smile as her head continually turned towards the aft deck.

Although he did not want to pry he was curious about their relationship. He knew Chase had many women the last few years but he felt there was something different about her as well as the way he reacted to her. She told him about her husband and her plan to go back to Wisconsin when her fall tours were over. He seemed shocked that she would be leaving Chase.

"I am afraid this is not 'forever after' like you had with Theresa. Not everyone finds someone as special as you did."

"Are you sure you have not found something special with Chase?"

Staring at him she said, "Truthfully I do not know how I am going to be able to leave him."

She realized she was finally admitting to herself that her feelings were much deeper than she had imagined.

"But I know he wants no long term commitments. I would never stay here in Seattle when he does not want me just so I could be near him. It will probably be the hardest thing I ever do but I have to leave at the end of October."

The morning seemed to speed by and the extensive lunch the restaurant had packed for them was a wonderful surprise. There were sandwiches and potato salad as well as fruit salad and cheese. Peanut butter cookies had been included for dessert. For Joe there was a bottle of wine and a six-pack of Hefeweizen with cut lemons for the two of them.

They anchored off shore of one of the islands they happened upon. After lunch Joe said he wanted to lie down for a nap. They concurred and headed for the bunks in the bow when Joe stopped them.

"I sleep in there. Why don't you two take the master suite?"

Staring at him she said, "But we cannot take your bedroom."

Returning a look at her, he said "I have not been able to sleep in there since Theresa died. Please take the bigger room."

Laying down on the waterbed together they knew they would not make love with Joe so close by. She liked the feeling of laying there with Chase's arms wrapped around her.

"Tell me about Theresa."

"There is not a whole lot to say. Theresa was short—probably only about five feet tall--and pretty pudgy. She was not what you would call good looking but she was beautiful to everyone who knew her. She exuded a radiance and there was always a twinkle in her eyes. And no one had a problem that Theresa could not solve or at least make them feel a little better after talking to her about it. One time I had a pretty nasty break up and I felt so much better after I told her my story. It is really hard to put a finger on what there was about her that made her so wonderful. But everyone who knew her loved her. She was like everyone's mother. Although Joe was devastated when she died there were so many others who also took her death hard. And she was as obsessed about boating and being on the water as you are."

She smiled when he said that. Sometimes just lying close to each other and talking to him was as enjoyable to her as making love. She knew she would miss being with him when she left on her tour. As they lay in Joe and Theresa's bed listening to the water splash against the outside of the boat they were lulled to sleep with their arms tightly wrapped around each other.

When they woke up Joe was taking the anchor up. It was time to head back. Nikki piloted the boat all the way back to the marina. She insisted that Joe put it in the berth. She knew she was not ready for such a big responsibility.

The next day they once again were on the dock at 7:00 a.m. Joe was busy stowing their lunch away. He knew it would not take Chase long to get the hang of piloting the boat and he took over the controls before the boat left the dock. She still had some paperwork to complete for her trip so she sat on the aft deck enjoying the day while completing her work.

Joe realized this was a repeat of yesterday with role reversal. This time Chase kept looking at Nikki. He was not able to take his eyes off of her any more than she had been able to keep her eyes off him the previous day.

Joe knew his friend cared a lot more for this woman than he was willing to admit. He felt sad that Chase seemed to be into such denial over his true feelings for Nikki.

"What are you going to do when she goes back to Wisconsin?"

"I don't know. Just go on as before. I have had a lot of relationships and it is sad when they end but life goes on."

"Do you think you will be able to give her up that easily? She is a very special woman."

Glancing at Joe, he said, "Nikki does not want any long term commitment. She has been too burned by her husband."

"Sometimes people do not know what they want."

"I do. I have my life and my condo and when I am not working, I can jump on my Harley and go anywhere when the mood strikes me. I am happy living the way I do."

Staring at him, Joe shook his head. Chase did not know it but he had a big surprise coming, and it would not be a happy one. Joe realized Chase had no idea how hard her leaving would hit him.

At lunch that day Nikki seemed very preoccupied. "Is there something wrong," Chase asked when she did not answer one of his questions.

Gazing at him, she realized he had asked her something.

"I am sorry. I guess I was thinking back. Today is the twentieth anniversary of my mother's death. I was thinking how it could not have possibly been that long ago."

They both turned when they heard Joe gasp beside them. As they glanced his way he said, "Today is the one year anniversary of my wife's death. I cannot believe she has been gone that long. I know there must be some reason God is keeping me on this earth when I only want to be with her. I am so glad you two said you would come out with me today. It would have been a very difficult day for me if you hadn't."

Giving him a big hug she replied sadly, "I will think of the two of you for the rest of my life on this day when I think of my mother."

Once again they retired to their cabins for an afternoon nap. This had been a very emotional day for all of them. As she lay wrapped in Chase's arms, she sighed. She wished with all her heart she could be with him like this for the rest of her life. She knew it was an impossible wish and a tear rolled down her face as she fell asleep.

When they awoke Chase piloted them back to the marina and docked the boat. Joe watched him with interest. He knew with his experience driving a motorcoach, he would catch on to the boat maneuvers in no time but Chase seemed to have a natural flair even Joe did not have.

After all the lines were tied and food gathered up they said good bye and walked hand in hand down the dock heading back to the condo. Tomorrow would be their last day together before their separate tours.

Chapter Forty

The two of them spent the day in his condo before going back to her houseboat after dinner. Nikki was pretty organized but needed to finish some last minute packing for her tour to the National Parks.

The flight to Las Vegas was leaving at noon on the following day. Since Chase had the day off he planned to drop her at the airport. He was not leaving until the following day so he wanted to spend some time with his mother that afternoon. He would be gone eight days and Nikki eleven so he would get back a couple of days before she did

Since it was Thursday night the big potluck party to welcome the weekend was in full swing. Nikki could not believe it. There had to be close to thirty people there. They had never had that many partygoers earlier in the season. Summer ending and the warmer temperatures must be bringing them out she thought.

She told Chase she had to make an appearance. She knew they wanted to be together since their time was winding down but these were her friends, and she knew they were curious about her companion. To her surprise Chase knew some of the people at the potluck and they starting catching up on old times while she talked to Brooke.

She wondered if the woman was still emailing

Brandon daily. The answer was "yes" and Brooke told her Brandon was definitely planning another visit soon since the White Sox were coming back to Seattle. This made her smile.

"I am so glad you have found someone to have as a friend. Brandon told me all about his dad. I do not mean to seem nosey but I know you were not very happy with your marriage. Sometimes you meet someone when you least expect it."

Blushing a little and hoping she had not said too much to Brandon about Chase, she wondered if maybe Brooke was also a little surprised to have found a friend. Her husband had been killed in a car accident four years previously. She had loved him dearly and had an extremely difficult time getting past his death.

Thinking about her upcoming trip she decided she better call her two sons this weekend before she lost her cell phone service in Utah. She had been so busy with Chase and her tours she knew she had not talked to her boys for a couple of weeks. Even though nothing changed with Ted, she liked to keep in touch with her sons. And she thought maybe she would try and feel Brandon out a little on his growing relationship with Brooke.

Before they realized it two hours had passed. Their eyes met across the deck and she knew it was time. He was giving her that hooded look of his. She had always assumed that men in their fifties lost some of their stamina but this was certainly not true of Chase. She could feel that ache returning to her stomach and knew they had to say their good-byes to the others soon.

It was another fifteen minutes before they made their way off the party boat and up to her houseboat. They barely made it in the door since she was circling her tongue around Chase's bottom and upper lips.

As they worked their way to the bedroom their clothes left a trail along the floor of the boat as she kept kissing him greedily. They almost missed the bed as he descended on top of her.

Marveling at their relationship he realized he had never been with a woman previously he wanted as frequently as he wanted her. It also amazed him the stamina he had at his age. He knew that definitely would not last forever.

He also felt something for her beyond the sexual even though he could not quite put his finger on what it was. He knew he would be sad when she left but supposed he would get over it. His life had always been about women entering and leaving.

The two of them did not get much sleep that night but she knew she could rest on the plane and sleep when she got to Vegas. Chase had said he would drive her to the airport and pick her up on the return. In that way she would not have to worry about parking her car for so many days at the airport or take the Super Shuttle..

Quickly it was morning and the two of them showered together before leaving for the airport. Knowing they would be apart so many days she had a hard time keeping her hands off of him. This morning for the first time she noticed he was constantly touching her, too.

As they drove to the airport it was difficult for her to keep her composure. She was thinking these next eleven days would be the longest in her life. She had no idea that he was thinking the same thing.

At least we will have almost two weeks together when I get back she thought. Chase's schedule could be more flexible than hers. He had chosen jobs for the fall when he knew she would also be out of town. Otherwise he had decided to bid on day jobs around the Seattle area when she would be there. He wanted their schedules to be as compatible as possible.

Pulling up in front of the airport departure door he took her suitcases out of the trunk and called for a skycap. As she hugged him good-bye she wrapped her arms around him and squeezed tight. This reminded her of that first hug she had given him at the San Francisco airport over a year ago. This time she could feel his body against hers. She suddenly broke the embrace and walked away quickly without looking back.

There were tears in her eyes as she boarded the plane. She told herself she had to get over this. There would be three more of these separations before the final one. She had received her fall schedule and she would have a Yellowstone trip after the National Parks. After that she had a Colorado train trip and finally a trip along the California coast from San Francisco to Los Angeles.

After her last tour there would be two weeks before the end of October. She had already given her notice on the houseboat. She wanted those last fourteen days with Chase but November first she would be on the road back to Wisconsin.

Her tour went well and she was really excited to see Sam again. The two of them ate their meals together and he talked about his family while she told him about her summer on the West Coast and her new friend, Joe. She also told him about Ted but never said anything about the new man in her life. She was trying not to think about Chase since it made it a little easier. She was not eating much and tossed and turned most nights.

Since the two of them were in remote areas they had decided not to call each other. She wondered how he was fairing. She assumed he probably was not as upset by the separation as she was. He was used to ending romances and since this was only a temporary relationship she decided he was probably doing just fine.

Surprisingly she had such wonderful passengers on this trip the time seemed to speed by. Before she knew it she was flying back to Seattle. Chase had told her he would wait in the bus holding area since they knew him there and would let him park if he stayed with his car.

Nikki paid for an airport cart since she had three pieces of luggage with her. As she rounded the corner to the bus parking lot she felt her heart jump. He was standing beside his car watching for her.

As soon as she saw him, she left her cart in the middle of the lot and ran to him. Their lips met greedily. She felt almost faint as he continued to kiss her.

They did not hear the chuckling behind them but he felt a tapping on his shoulder. As he broke their kiss he saw the parking lot attendant laughing with Nikki's luggage cart in his hands.

"I think you forgot your bags," he said as he smiled at the two of them.

Normally she would have been embarrassed by the situation but all she could focus on was being with Chase again.

As she looked closer at him, she noticed he looked a little gaunt. She wondered if he had missed her more than he wanted to acknowledge. She knew he would never admit it to her, especially considering he would not admit it to himself.

"Have you been eating all right?"

"I have been okay. I think I had a touch of the flu."

That sounded a little odd to her but she knew she would not get any more out of him so she let it go.

They decided to go to his condo since he lived close to the airport. Her luggage never made it out of the car that night. Not eating much on her tour and since Chase kept her busy throughout the rest of the evening she started getting hunger pangs in the middle of the night.

At 3:00 a.m. she got up and fixed eggs. Following her to the kitchen Chase ate three fried eggs, five pieces of bacon, hash browns and three pieces of toast. She had never seen him eat so much.

With a secret smile she looked at him and said, "You must be feeling better from your flu."

Nodding at her as he kept eating she just shook her head.

Chapter Forty-One

They had a few days together before her next tour but she knew she was too busy to go anywhere with him. She needed to get ready for her Yellowstone trip and the following Friday Brandon was planning another visit to see Brooke and his White Sox. Her other son, Kyle, had not been able to visit all summer so at the last minute he decided to come at the same time. It would be a family reunion for all of them.

She was not sure how her sons would feel about Chase but since it was not anything permanent she thought everything would be alright. She decided to talk to the boys about Chase before they visited her. She was not sure how much Brooke had told Brandon about his mother's friend.

After speaking to her sons they seemed to be fine with the fact that she had a friend in her life. They knew she was probably lonely, especially with their father no longer cognizant. They knew she was still planning on coming home the first part of November so they did not think it was anything too serious.

Neither of them thought she was in a long lasting relationship and they knew their mother would never divorce their dad. Besides they were happy with the emotional support she was getting out of her relationship with Chase.

Her sons were happy she had someone to talk to who was in the same line of work and understood her job related stresses. Because of her age they never dreamed she was in a sexual relationship. As her children they thought she was too old for that.

Nikki hoped Chase would enjoy being with her boys. She knew he had never had a desire to have children but he was as much of a sports fanatic as her sons. She felt that would give all of them common ground.

The good news was that he had bought the tickets for the weekend Sox games with the Mariners and her sons and Brooke would be going to the games with him. He had even bought an extra ticket for Sunday's game for Joe.

Once again alternating between their two homes they even had time to spend all day Wednesday with Joe on his boat. They were both starting to think of him like a dad since both of them had lost their fathers.

They understood how much Joe missed Theresa everyday but he had also started looking forward to his time spent with the two of them. Chase had caught on right away to all the nuances of piloting and she was getting better at handling the boat, too.

Before she knew it Thursday night had arrived and her boys were flying in. Chase was not sure about going along with her to pick up her sons but she insisted so he rode with her to the airport. Because of the time change her sons would be arriving at 6:00 p.m.

Since it was Thursday she knew the potluck evening would be going on. She planned that they would be able to eat dinner at the party especially since she knew Brandon was looking forward to seeing Brooke as quickly as possible.

As soon as her sons got in the car they started talking about their upcoming weekend of games and players. Naturally Chase, like Brooke, was rooting for the

Mariners. By the time they got to the marina the three of them were having friendly arguments over who were the best players. She knew the weekend of baseball games would be a fun time for all of them.

Chase was feeling a little uncomfortable at first and did not want to stay at the party. However Kyle was ready to talk sports and since Brandon had gone to see Brooke, he knew he should stay for a while and talk to Nikki's son. It did not take long for him to realize he liked both of her sons. Before he knew it he was relaxing around them as if he had known them forever.

Even though he would miss his alone time with their mother, he had a feeling he was in for a nice weekend with the boys there. Chase could sense they also enjoyed his company. Nikki's son Kyle worked for a company in Milwaukee that made all the chrome for Harleys. So after they had exhausted their sports discussion they begin talking about motorcycles.

The weekend passed quickly. While everyone was at the baseball games Nikki worked on preparing for her tour. When the games were not going on they took the boys and Brooke all over the city to show them the sites. Since there was a game on Sunday afternoon her sons had decided to fly back home on Monday.

Joe went with the four of them to the game Sunday afternoon and then Nikki met them at his boat. He had the restaurant prepare them a nice meal and they took a short ride in the Sound while eating dinner aboard.

The next morning she began packing for her tour. She was leaving on Tuesday afternoon and since she and Chase had not slept together the whole weekend they had decided she would go to his condo after she dropped the boys at the airport. Once again he would take her to the airport like he had for her National Parks tour.

Brandon said good-bye to Brooke. Nikki had a feeling the romance was progressing well but was not sure with the distance involved if anything serious would develop. On the way to the airport she stopped at a restaurant so her sons could have a nice breakfast and then afterwards they went to a sandwich shop to get some food for the four-hour plane ride home.

Although sad that her boys were leaving she knew she would see them in less than two months. Besides she was anxious to get back to Chase.

When she arrived at the condo his car was in the garage but he did not answer when she called out his name. She pulled her overnight bag out of the car and took it into his bedroom. She suddenly realized why he had not answered her.

He was lying in his bed naked with the sheets pulled back waiting for her. In less than thirty seconds she was undressed and laying in his arms. At that moment there was nowhere else she would rather have been.

Chapter Forty-Two

Chase dropped her at the airport the next day. Once again she had not gotten much sleep but every moment she spent with him seemed precious to her since their time together was winding down.

She hugged him hard like the last time and realized these partings were not getting any easier. She quickly turned and walked into the terminal. He had a couple of day jobs lined up and then an eight-day tour into Canada. Once again they decided not to call each other. She knew hearing the sound of his voice when they were so far apart would hurt too much.

The Yellowstone trip was fun right from the start. She flew into Salt Lake City. This had always been one of her favorite cities. She could sense the history as she walked down the streets of this town. There were forty-eight passengers on this tour so she would be kept very busy.

She had not been on this trip for two years but she would have another favorite driver, Jason. She and her driver had done this tour together three times previously and they always worked well as a team.

As they climbed through the Wasatch Mountains heading for Jackson, Wyoming, she knew the passengers were in for a real treat. They would spend two days in

Jackson and she loved watching as the first sight of the Teton Mountains came into view. It always took her travelers breath away.

After leaving Jackson they would spend two nights at Yellowstone's Old Faithful Lodge before finally ending up in Rapid City, South Dakota and the Black Hills. What she liked most about this tour was how different the mountain ranges looked at each of their stops.

She and her driver had lots of catching up to do. Over the years they would email each other from time to time and she was always interested in his new girlfriends. He seemed to have an endless supply in and out of his life just like Chase.

It was hard for drivers to have a normal relationship when they were on the road so many days every year. Jason use to tell her his cat hardly recognized him when he would show up at home.

Once again, she had terrific passengers and the tour seemed to fly by. Although she missed Chase it was easier when she was on the road to try and not think of him too much. And she would often be too busy to dwell on their relationship. Nights, of course, were different. Not only would she lie awake thinking about him but she missed having his arms around her.

And there were always little reminders of him. In Jackson she was walking down the street and looked up to see the Starbucks shop right in front of her. In Yellowstone a motorcoach from Chase's company went driving by. In Rapid City she saw a man who had that same kind of smile in his eyes that Chase had. By the time she saw the man in Rapid City all she could think about was getting back to him.

Finally it was time for her to go back to Seattle, a place she was beginning to think of as home. She knew she had to quit those thoughts. The flight from Rapid City into Denver was smooth but then she had a couple of hour's layover before her next flight.

Chase would still be out on his trip for one more day so after she landed back at the Emerald City she took a shuttle to her houseboat. It was 10:00 p.m. before she managed to get herself and all her luggage on the boat. She saw Brooke briefly and said a quick hello before storing her luggage and going to bed.

The following morning she got up early. She needed to get unpacked and clean her clothes. There was only five days before her next trip to Colorado to ride the trains. In between washing her clothes she started working on her kit for the next tour. She decided to leave her suitcases out and repack when her clothes were washed.

Since Chase would not get back into town until late he told her he would be over in the morning. She was so tired by 9:00 p.m. she climbed into bed and fell instantly asleep. She was having a very vivid dream of being held by Chase.

The kisses felt so real she trembled. This had never happened before. All of a sudden she opened her eyes and realized she was wrapped in his arms. He had come to the boat instead of going home. Obviously he needed to be with her as much as she needed him. She touched his cheek with her hand and sighed. How was she ever going to leave him in November she wondered?

The next morning he went to his condo to do a few things and she finished up her trip preparation and packing. When he came back that evening he told her Joe wanted them to go out with him overnight in the boat. She did not care what they did as long as she was with him.

Once again he stayed overnight with her on the houseboat. The next morning they got up extremely early.

They had to go across town and would get caught in some of the morning rush hour. She threw a few things into an overnight bag and they made it to the pier at 7:00 a.m. ready to go.

Joe came out of the inside cabin. He had just finished unpacking the food for the trip.

"I have some bad news. I am having some plumbing problems in the restaurant and I don't feel comfortable leaving while that is going on."

The two of them told him that was okay and perhaps they could do the overnight when Nikki got back from her next tour.

"No, no," Joe replied. They looked at him. "I want you two to go without me."

"But we cannot go overnight on your boat without you."

"Yes you can and you will. All the food has been prepared and ready and I have complete confidence in both yours and Chase's ability to pilot this boat around the Sound."

Staring at Joe a little strangely Chase wondered how big the plumbing problem really was.

As Joe said good-bye the two of them went in and unpacked their belongings. They noticed the boat had been filled with fuel and more food than they could possibly eat in two days. As the boat cruised out of the marina they saw Joe waving at them from the dock and they waved back.

"Where do you think we should go?"

"If it is okay with you, I want to pick a place to go. Next time we go out you can pick the destination."

That sounded fair to her but she was curious where he would take her.

He already knew where he was going. He had told Joe his plan since he wanted the man to know where his boat would be and he had thought it sounded like a great idea.

As she was fixing sandwiches for their lunch she heard the anchor being lowered. She went up on deck to see where they were. They were anchored off Orcas Island and the little cabin could be seen in the distance.

"This place is perfect. Thank you for thinking of it."

"I thought if we could not be in the cabin at least this would be the second best place for us to be. I have so many happy memories of us in that cabin I just wanted to be close to it."

Putting her arms around him, she kissed him passionately.

"Let me go wrap up the sandwiches. I suppose we should go to the bedroom since it is daylight and the hot tub is on the outside."

They never left the cove. The two of them finally ate their sandwiches and that evening once again he sliced lemons for their beer before sinking into the hot tub with her.

It was the middle of the night when she awoke Chase had his arms wrapped around her. She began stroking his face and tears started forming in her eyes. He was now used to instantly awakening when she touched him at night.

"Why are you crying?"

"I guess I am so happy when I am with you and since our time together is almost over I just felt overwhelmed."

Feeling a sharp pain go through his heart he held her tighter.

Before they knew it their time was up. They pulled into the marina about 6:00 p.m. Joe was waiting for them. He came onto the boat to help them get the food off. While he was standing by the wheel he looked at his fuel gauge.

"I guess you two did not go too far," Joe said with a twinkle in his eyes.

"How's your plumbing?

"The problem was solved rather quickly."

As soon as they took the extra food and supplies into the restaurant Chase drove Nikki back to the houseboat. They spent the night there and then the next morning went back to his place. Once again she brought along all her things for the tour. She had some calls to make and he had to go into his office for a little while but otherwise they spent the day together.

When he returned they took the Harley to lunch. This time they went south of the city. There was a restaurant he liked in Tacoma and since it was such a beautiful day they both looked forward to the ride.

After returning from lunch they decided to take a nap. Nikki knew this would be a typical pre-night trip evening. If she knew Chase, and she knew him very well now, they would not be getting much rest tonight. It seemed like both of them had a hard time sleeping when they were going to be apart and they often talked long into the night.

Lately she was learning how to sleep on planes. He had a five-day tour the next week and a couple of day jobs so he would be waiting at the airport on her return from Colorado.

Once again their time together sped by. As he dropped her at the airport she told him she would see him in nine days. As usual she hugged him tightly and then turned and walked into the terminal. Leaving him at the airport never got any easier. As she went through security she had to wipe the tears from her eyes. She did not know he was also wiping tears from his eyes as he left the airport.

Chapter Forty-Three

Nikki remembered Dean, the bad driver on her train trip the previous year. This time she knew things would go well. Jason's company in Denver handled all her company's train and Yellowstone tours. She had requested him for the trip and when they were together in Yellowstone he had told her the tour had been assigned to him.

She was not able to spend a lot of time talking with Jason on this trip since he was constantly deadheading to the next train stop. On day four they pulled into Durango about 6:00 p.m. The travelers were on their own for dinner that night since they had a hot meal at the train stop on top of the mountain for lunch that day.

They dropped their passengers downtown and told them they would pick them up at 8:30 p.m. Finding a street to park the bus they walked three blocks to a restaurant lounge that he knew.

Knowing the travelers would not find their "hideout" would give them some down time alone. Jason was not real hungry because he also had a big lunch. Since they were still on duty they did not have any alcohol but they ordered a sandwich to share.

"There is something different about you, Nikki. You seem unhappy to me and I did not notice that about you on our Yellowstone tour."

As she looked at Jason, she could not believe he could sense how bad she felt. She thought she was keeping her feelings under control. This was only an eight-day tour but for some reason being away from Chase seemed harder this time than ever before. She knew it was probably better that she talk to someone and her driver seemed perfect since he had told her about his girlfriends over the years.

"I have a friend. He drives a motorcoach in Seattle. We have been together since July."

Then she told him about her husband. He could not believe all the problems she had in her life in the two years since he had last driven with her. He was very happy she had found someone she cared for.

"But it is not going to last."

She then told him her plan for going back to Wisconsin at the end of October.

"How can he let you go like that?"

"He cannot commit. He never has and never will. I won't stay out in Seattle under those conditions because I do not want him to think I am clinging to him. He has to want to be with me. And, I do not believe he wants to be with anyone in a long-term relationship. I try not to think about leaving him because I have only realized in just the last few days that I could live with him forever. I guess that is why you noticed how sad I am feeling."

"You are doing the right thing. As hard as it is, you need to leave him now before it becomes even harder for you. You will feel hurt but it will be a lot worse the longer you wait. Trust me. And, Nikki, listen to me! Be thankful for all the moments you shared. You know I have a lot of experience in this area."

For some reason her talk with Jason made her feel much better. Possibly just telling someone how she really felt about Chase made her decision to leave him more real and more acceptable. She felt as if an immense burden had been lifted from her.

As they were leaving the restaurant she gave him a big hug. She did not want the passengers to see her hug him like that because they might get the wrong impression. But she knew what he had told her was right and she appreciated his opinion.

"Thank you, Jason. You will never know how much you helped me."

As they walked back to the coach she noticed he had a big smile on his face.

The rest of the time sped by. Before she realized it they were dropping everyone at the airport for their return trips home. She noticed a few of the men had misty eyes. She was not sure what it was about this particular vacation that made men so emotional but it happened almost every time she did this particular tour.

It was now time to go back to Seattle. She was really excited. She now felt so much better since her talk with Jason. There was only twelve days before her last tour down the California coast. She knew she was going to treasure every precious moment she had left being with Chase.

After she returned from the tour down the coast, she would still have two weeks before leaving him. She also would have no responsibilities except to pack her things for the trip back to Wisconsin. She needed to be with him as much as time allowed. She wanted as many sweet memories as possible to take back home with her.

Even though her heart would ache for him, she would always carry the love she had for him in her whole being. There were many people in the world who never had a chance at love like she had with Chase.

Instead of being sad she would be thankful for every

day she had been given with him. She had come to terms with the changes that would take place in her life. She knew when she left Seattle she would lose something of tremendous value to her and would never be able to replace what they had together. For some reason she was meant to journey alone but some how she would learn to accept her fate.

This time when she spotted Chase in the bus holding area she did not run to him as before. She only had two suitcases and she walked very surely towards him. She had a gleam in her eye and he sensed there was something different about her. It was Chase who walked quickly towards her and grabbed her tightly. Just before their lips met she smiled. She knew when she left him, he would never forget her.

Chapter Forty-Four

Chase had decided to do some day work the next four days. He could make more money being on the road but he wanted to be with her as much as possible when she was in town. Since this was his company's busy season he could have been working every day and they were not real happy with him. But he insisted he have the time off from the overnight tours.

Once he made up his mind he packed a few things and moved in with her on the houseboat. Since he had to work every day he did not want to be shuffling between their homes. She was surprised because this was a big step for him to not stay at his home when he was in town.

However, he felt it would be easier for her to prepare for her last tour down the coast if she stayed on the boat where all her tour things were located. He wanted her to finish all her pre-tour work while he worked his day jobs. That way they could spend the upcoming week together without any distractions.

Joe asked them to spend the weekend on his boat and this time he would accompany them. He would give them privacy when they needed it but he missed having them in his life and told Chase that selfishly he needed them, too.

Chase was fine with that. He liked having Joe

around and sensed it was important that he be with them for the weekend. He also wanted some time to have Nikki all to himself. So he had talked to his friend and had been told they could use the cabin again on Orcas Island.

Telling Joe they would meet him on Friday afternoon they agreed he would drop them off at the island late on Sunday. He would then come back the following Thursday to pick them up.

That would give her Friday for the last minute details she needed to handle since she was flying to San Francisco on the following Saturday afternoon. He knew she needed some time to pack and make some final calls since her tour started on Sunday and it was sometimes hard to reach suppliers on the weekend.

Telling her to pack for a week he would not tell her where they were going.

"It is my surprise." When you come back from your tour down the coast we will have two weeks together before you leave for Wisconsin. You plan what you want to do and then you can surprise me."

She was happy he had said that since she had already decided where she wanted to go. And nothing would have changed her mind. She had even told Joe her plan.

Joe loved being in on the planning of the surprises they were giving each other. He knew when she left there would be some very bad times ahead for both of them. However he had a feeling it was going to be much worse for Chase.

Noticing the subtle difference in her, he realized she had reached acceptance. Chase, however, was definitely still in the denial stage and Joe had a feeling he would need him. Losing Nikki to Wisconsin would be like losing a loved one to death. He knew she had made up her mind to never see Chase again once she left Seattle. And in a way, he agreed. To do anything else would be too painful for either of them.

Joe finally came to the understanding this was the reason God was keeping him from Theresa. His unfinished work was helping Nikki and Chase. He also knew it would not be much longer and he would be with his beloved forever.

Once again they fell into a routine. He would arrive at the houseboat after work about 6:00 p.m. and she would have dinner ready. Chase liked to cook and she liked it when he took his turn. But for these four days she did not want him to spend time on anything but her.

Every night she watched for the Harley to pull up. He stopped at a market by the marina each evening before he got there and bought her a small bouquet of flowers. It reminded her of two years ago when she watched those men after work in the marketplace buying flowers to take to their wives or girlfriends.

She loved that he brought her flowers but she also kept telling him they would die when they went on the boat with Joe. He told her to take them over to Brooke's before they left. He just liked to see her face light up when he gave her a bouquet each night.

Chase would shower as soon as arrived at the boat. She decided it was her duty to make sure his back was clean. She knew there were some areas he might have trouble reaching otherwise.

After the time spent in the shower they would eat dinner and then sit on the outside deck and watch the sunset. They would hold hands and she would put her head on his shoulder. It always reminded her of the first time they had sat like that at the riverside park in Portland. She knew she was storing memories for her return to Wisconsin.

They always went to bed as soon as the sun had

set. They needed to be with each other but she knew he needed some sleep since he would leave early for work each morning.

Time passed swiftly as it always seemed to when they were with each other but this time they knew they were headed on another journey.

The three of them sailed all over the Sound that weekend. They were both becoming very proficient at handling the cabin cruiser and Joe felt comfortable with their abilities.

Every afternoon Joe would take a nap. They also went to their bedroom at that time but napping was not a high priority. Their lovemaking seemed sweeter now. Both of them were experts at sensing what the other one needed and wanted.

In the evening Joe would turn in early and they spent many hours in the hot tub on the deck before retiring to the waterbed. Some nights they spent talking but some evenings they just sat in the hot tub holding hands and saying nothing as they looked skyward.

Many nights she wondered what it would be like if they were together all the time. Maybe life would not seem this idyllic if they were with each other every day. However since she knew that was never going to happen she let the thought go.

Sunday afternoon arrived and she could not believe Chase's surprise. She did not think they would ever have time to go back to the cabin again. As Joe dropped them at the marina she had tears in her eyes as she waved good-bye to him.

Chase turned to look at her and saw the tears and had to turn away. He felt his eyes misting, too. He could not believe how emotional he got around her. That had definitely never happened to him before.

As usual they fell into their old routine. They would walk in the morning on the beach, lunch at one of the restaurants, make love before their nap, and spend hours talking after dinner.

He told her how he had always wanted to have his own small company with two or three motorcoaches. There were a lot of group leaders in the Seattle area who would work with a small company that was reliable and honest.

He had a couple of driver friends and they had talked about running their own company someday. However the cost was prohibitive since the average motorcoach cost around five hundred thousand and there was no way they could ever get that kind of financing. He realized it was just a dream like Nikki wanting a cabin cruiser. Just like her, he realized it never hurt to have a dream even if it was unattainable.

"The day we stop dreaming is the day we die, Chase."

She was reminded of a phrase she had just read. "The more you and your partner grow, the more you find each other fascinating." She was discovering many new facets of his personality through their talks and she was finding him much more complex than he let on. Her next thought was would it be so bad if she had fallen for him? She knew the answer to that without voicing it.

Thursday afternoon came quickly and before they knew it Joe was back at the dock ready to pick them up. He was very sad when he saw the two of them. Realizing time was running out he wished there was something he could do to help them stay together. However he had a bad feeling it was not meant to be.

Chapter Forty-Five

This would be Nikki's last tour while out on the West Coast and she was happy but at the same time sad. She had worked hard to make money to help with Ted's expenses but she was getting tired from all her travels. She was sad because it would not be long before she would be leaving her houseboat and more importantly, Chase.

This was the last time he would drop her at the airport. Once again she had tears in her eyes as she went through security. But she had no idea that he also had tears in his eyes as he drove away from her.

This would be a bittersweet tour. She would start in San Francisco and she knew it would feel strange to be in that town without him.

This was a nine-day tour and since her company used the same hotel in San Francisco for this trip as the Pacific Coast journey, she knew she would not be able to stop thinking of him. It actually turned out even harder when she discovered her room was only a few doors from where she and Chase had connecting rooms on their last tour together in this city.

Her company used a Los Angeles based motorcoach company since the trip ended there. The driver she had used before had retired so now she would have to break in someone new.

Luckily when she met her driver, Brian, she knew things would be fine. He was a little younger than most of the usual drivers and seemed very friendly and competent. Most tour managers liked the younger drivers because they worked much harder. Younger drivers could get on the better tours if tour managers requested them, so many of these drivers would do extra things to please their tour manager.

Her passengers were ready to have a good time as was usual. Starting a tour in San Francisco was also nice because travelers always looked forward to coming to this town. There was the usual city tour with Chris as her guide, a boat ride on the bay, and shopping time before dinner that evening on the Wharf.

The next morning they would drive to Yosemite. There were a couple of National Parks that she particularly liked and Yosemite was at the top of the list. After their stay at that park, the tour would continue down the coast through Monterey, Carmel, a stop at the Hearst Castle, and into Los Angeles and Hollywood.

Sometimes it was hard for her to decide which of the two coast tours she liked the best. Anytime she could drive down the Pacific Coast either in Oregon or California she was happy. To her the tours always seemed to go fast since there were always so many new sights each day. However she felt she liked the other tour best because she could do it with Chase. She only wished he could be the one who was driving her down the Pacific Coast right now.

She had mixed feelings on this tour. Part of her wanted the trip to be over so she could get back to Chase. The other part of her knew how quickly those last two weeks with him would fly by and so she was ready to delay the start of their last days together.

All too soon her tour was over and Brian was

dropping everyone at the airport for their return trips home. She thanked him for all his help and told him she would definitely enjoy working with him again.

Now it was time to go home. She knew that Chase had done his final tour through the Canadian Rockies for the year while she was on her trip and he was returning the day before her.

For the final time she saw him waiting for her in the bus holding area. They both seemed to squeeze each other a little harder than usual. She realized this would be the last time they would meet as they were now doing.

Taking her back to the houseboat he still had one more day job the next day. Then he was taking a couple of weeks off to be with her before she left. Since the busy time was now winding down his company did not mind him taking time off. He stayed with her that evening and when he left the next morning she reminded him that she would not get to his condo until later in the evening. She had a few things to do before their trip started and she did not want him worrying about her like he had the last time when she had gotten delayed by the accident.

He was planning on going home after work and packing his bags. She had not told him where she was taking him except that they would be on the water for ten days and he would need to pack warmer clothes. Since the boat was near his place it made more sense for them to stay at his house that evening.

Busy all that day washing her clothes and packing up, she decided not to haul everything back to Wisconsin in the car. She packed up six boxes containing her tour things and some unneeded clothes and took them to the local mailbox store to be shipped back home.

Calling Kyle, she let him know when the shipment would arrive. She wanted him to store the boxes in her garage until the renters left. Then he could move them in the house after the cleaners had gone through the house.

She felt relieved getting that job finished. It would be one less thing to worry about before leaving. She wanted as much time as possible with Chase these last few days.

Buying some groceries for their trip she took the food and clothes to the boat and unpacked everything. She had not told him but she was having dinner with Joe. She knew she was going to miss the man who had become like a father to her and she wanted to spend some extra time alone with him.

As they were eating they talked a little about the upcoming trip. She had decided she wanted to visit Victoria and then spend the rest of their days together circling Vancouver Island. Joe had done some research for her and gave her advice on where to stop and places where they should visit. He had even helped her make docking arrangements at the ports she wanted to stay at.

If she had not been leaving Seattle, and more importantly Chase, she told Joe she wished he could have come on the trip with them. He asked her if she thought she would come back to Washington next year even though he already guessed the answer. Shaking her head "no" she told him she would never come back.

"I could not go through this again. It would hurt too much. I need to walk away and stay away. Besides if I ever came back I do not think I would be strong enough to leave him a second time. And that is not what he wants."

"How do you know he doesn't want you to stay with him forever?"

"If he wanted me to stay he would have mentioned something about a future together. He never has. He just thinks his life will go on when I leave. He does not have any idea that he is not only in my heart but also a part of my soul now. I cannot think of anyone I would rather grow old with. At least as we journey on alone my love for him will always be with me. I will always remember what we had with each other until the day I die."

Joe understood how she finally reached acceptance when she told him about her talk with Jason in Colorado. She realized many people never experienced what she and Chase had together and she had to be happy for the few months they shared.

"I am so thankful for every day I have had with him. It has been a precious gift I was given. Eventually the sadness will be replaced by the happy memories."

Joe told her that he wanted her to keep in touch with him and as they left the boat she hugged him extra hard and told him how much knowing him had meant to her. She knew she would miss him being a part of her life. She truly felt she was losing her father all over again.

They both had tears in their eyes as they walked out of the restaurant to the parking lot.

Chapter Forty-Six

It was nearly 9:00 p.m. by the time she got to Chase's place. Even though he knew she was coming later, nevertheless he seemed worried about her. She told him she had wanted to take her things to the boat and that she had spent some time with Joe.

"I cannot tell you how much I will miss him when I leave. I feel he is a part of my family."

He told her he felt the same way about Joe.

"It is a little sad that I have been going into that restaurant for several years and never realized what a terrific man he is. He has been like a father to both of us. I wish I had known him better a long time ago. I know he will not be around forever and my life will not be the same when he is gone."

Nikki gave him a strange look when he made that statement. She wondered why he could not say the same thing about her. Insightfully she realized he was thinking if he did not talk about her leaving it would be easier for him to deal with the situation.

She knew by his actions that he cared for her but he had never once said anything about his feelings towards her and she was very hurt by that. She was not asking for any long term commitment but she did want him to say how much she had meant to him.

She had to let these thoughts go. It would drive her crazy if she started dwelling on what he thought or did not think about her. In her heart she realized he believed she would be coming back to Seattle next summer and before she departed she was going to tell him that was not going to happen. When she left this city it would be forever. She was never coming back.

Now it was time for them to enjoy the next few days together. She was going to store every precious memory in her heart of these last few days spent with him.

"I want to get an early start tomorrow. Are you ready for bed," she asked with a twinkle in her eye?

"I cannot think of a better place to be right now."

They had been together long enough she knew every inch of his body and what he liked best. What was even more exciting was he knew her body, too, and always made sure she was satisfied before he was. She had a feeling when she went away she would ache for him for a long time.

It was almost 7:30 a.m. when the boat left the dock the following morning. Joe was there to wave good-bye to them. They all had tears in their eyes thinking about this being Nikki and Chase's last journey together. No more "journeys ahead" she thought with a sadness she had a hard time shaking.

They arrived in Victoria by 4:30 p.m. They would be spending two nights here since they both thought it would be fun to spend some time exploring the city.

She remembered touring Victoria in the eighties and she had tried to tease her husband about moving to this city at the time. Naturally practical Ted had reminded her that this town was in Canada and she should get any thought of living there out of her head. It had just been a passing thought; one she was not really considering. Sometimes Ted made her so angry with his realistic approach to life.

She wondered if he had ever had any hopes or dreams in his lifetime.

She knew many Americans lived in this wonderful city. All they did was take the ferry back to Seattle every six months to keep their citizenship status up to date. She did not think she would like to have to hassle with that situation but it was without doubt a beautiful place to visit.

Victoria did not get the rain Seattle did. Since the temperature was moderate most of the year there were colorful flowers everywhere throughout the city which were either planted in the ground or hanging in large baskets all over town. It gave the place a feeling of welcome whenever one visited.

They had dinner overlooking the water in the inner harbor not far from where they had docked Joe's boat. The restaurant had outside seating and they watched all the people walking by as they ate. They finished their meal and got back to the boat just in time to watch the sunset.

Since it was October, the temperatures cooled down more rapidly in the evening. There were also very few boats at the marina and none anchored close to them. With a wink she told Chase to go slice a lemon. She was just immersing herself into the hot tub when he came back with their two mugs of Hefeweizen. It took him twenty seconds to put the mugs down, undress, and lower himself in the water next to her. He had broken her previous record of thirty seconds!

The next day they went on a tour of Butchart Gardens and other sites around the city in the red double-decker buses from London. The Victoria tour company had ties to Chase's motorcoach company and they let them tour for free. Naturally they both tipped the driver guide extremely well! The tour ended at a downtown hotel for high tea.

After tea the two of them walked back to the marina hand in hand and sat on the outside deck until after sunset. They were not talking as much as they use to. It was as if they knew since the future ahead was empty for them there was no need to talk about their wishes or dreams anymore.

It was a very bittersweet time. She noticed, however, they were constantly touching each other in some way. She knew even though he never said anything he did not want to let go anymore than she did.

Many times while touring the city that day she had felt him behind her as if he wanted to encircle her in his arms and never let go. It was a very strange sensation since he never touched her but she knew if she stepped backwards she would have been in his arms.

She knew if he asked her to stay with him she would never leave Seattle. There was nothing in Wisconsin for her except her sons. Besides, Brandon might eventually end up in Washington if his romance with Brooke continued as it was. He was a teacher and he could be mobile if he wanted to be.

Kyle eventually was planning to move to the Reno/Lake Tahoe area if he could get a job in computers in one of the big casinos. He only had two more years before he would be vested in his Milwaukee Company and then he wanted to leave.

Having recently receiving a report about Ted, the doctors said that some of his body functions appeared to be shutting down. Although this type of coma patient could live quite a long time, Ted's doctors did not think that would be the case with the recent change in his condition.

Only time would tell about her husband. Since he no longer was aware of his surroundings she knew it would not matter to Ted where she lived. She just needed to make enough money to keep up his expensive care.

Thinking about her life she realized there was no reason she could not stay with Chase in Seattle forever. Well there was one reason. Chase did not want her to stay. And there was no way she would force herself upon him.

After they made love that evening, she lay in his arms thinking about their relationship. Sometimes she had a hard time not feeling a little upset with him over his refusal to say anything about her leaving him.

He fell asleep that night with his arms wrapped tightly around her. As the boat rocked in the water, she felt the tears run down her face. The thought of never sleeping with his arms around her again was almost more than she could bear.

The next morning they were up early and her dark thoughts from the evening before had dissipated. The sun was shining brightly and they were both ready for the next leg of their excursion.

Chapter Forty-Seven

As they continued their journey up the western side of Vancouver Island they passed Ladysmith and Vancouver. Neither of them was interested in stopping at Vancouver. She had been there a couple of times before and he was in the city several times a year on tour.

From there they traveled all the way to Cumberland before docking at a marina near that city for the evening. They ate dinner on the boat and watched the sunset before retiring for their evening of lovemaking.

The next day they continued north up the eastern side of the island. They passed the town of Campbell River and onto the Port Hardy area. Joe had arranged for them to dock at a marina in a little town called Bear Cove.

This trip seemed like an idyllic life to her. Cruising and stopping in one different port after the other was just as much fun as she had imagined. And it seemed like the people they met at the different marinas were always very friendly and helpful.

Chase did not care where they were as long as he was with her. She would catch herself daydreaming about making little trips like this with him for the rest of their lives. Then she would force herself back to reality. She wondered what he was thinking. For the past few months she had often read his mind but on this trip he had been so quiet she did not know what was going through his head. She wondered if maybe he was just ready to let her go.

On the fifth day they had a shorter day. Today they would go around the top part of Vancouver Island to Winter Harbor. As they rounded that part of the island they would then start traveling south on the Pacific Ocean.

When they left Winter Harbor there would be a long run to Ucluelet since there were only a few towns on this side of the island and hardly any roads. Most places on the Pacific side were only accessed by boat or seaplane.

They were both hoping the weather would hold. They had been lucky enough so far to be experiencing an Indian summer but you never knew how long that would last. Being out on the open ocean could get rough and although she had absolute confidence in Chase's abilities to handle the boat she wanted these last memories to be peaceful ones.

After conferring with the owners of the marina they decided to spend an extra day in Winter Harbor. The port was tucked into a cove and since the weatherman was calling for a quick storm to come through the area they thought it would be more comfortable and safe staying there a little longer.

The two of them were in bed when the storm hit. Since they were on a generator they did not have to worry about losing power. However the storm was much worse than either of them had anticipated. Thank goodness they had decided to stay over.

Chase decided he needed to go check his lines. Joe had taught both of them how to tie the boat down but with all the rocking he decided he needed to make sure everything was secure.

Wanting to go outside with him to help he told her there was no sense in both of them getting drenched. It seemed like forever before he got back. One of the lines had become loose in the storm and as he tightened the rope he had fallen on the slippery deck and hit his head. He had a gash on his forehead and it was bleeding.

Helping him out of his wet clothes she cleaned the wound and put on bandages from the first aid kit. She was thankful the cut was not deep enough to need stitches. She teased him that now he would have a scar as a reminder of her.

She quickly discovered he was upset by her remark by the tone in his voice when he got into bed. He put the covers over his body and laid with his back to her. This was the first time he had ever gone to bed not facing her!

It only took a minute for her to realize he was in deep denial over her leaving. He had never come to the acceptance she had. She quickly said a little prayer of thanks that Joe would be there for him when she left.

His behavior did not make it any easier on her. Knowing she could not sleep since she was upset by his actions she went to the main cabin and started reading her book. She did not want to say anything to him for fear of saying something she would later regret. She realized getting past her anger at the way he totally ignored what was happening to their relationship was becoming more and more difficult for her.

She understood he had commitment problems before they started their affair. However Joe had told her that he knew Chase loved her. The problem was he would not admit it to himself. She could not understand why he could not voice his feelings to her. There was no way with his unspoken actions that he could not feel as deeply for her as she did for him. It was hard to comprehend why he could not admit to himself that what they had together was a very powerful and wonderful relationship.

She only read for about ten minutes when he came out of the bedroom looking for her. He was rubbing his forehead as if he had a headache.

"Aren't you coming to bed? I cannot sleep without you."

She looked at him and sighed. The thought passed through her head that if he could not sleep without her tonight what would he do when she was gone forever back to Wisconsin?

Not wanting to put any strain on the time they had left together she closed her book and followed him back to the waterbed. He wrapped his arms around her and quickly fell asleep. She, however, lay there most of the night unable to sleep. It was almost five hours later when she finally closed her eyes. Her dreams were filled with storms and blood and her head was pounding by the time morning arrived.

It was a good thing that the two of them had decided to spend an extra day at Winter Harbor. Her stomach was upset along with her headache and after changing his dressing she told him she needed to go back to bed and rest for awhile.

There were still dark clouds in the sky and the sea was very rough. He decided to walk through town while she went back to bed. When he returned to the boat she was sound asleep. He entered the bedroom and sitting down in a chair looked at her while she lay sleeping. As he watched her he began to understand how much she meant to him. He had never felt this way about someone before.

He had feelings he could not understand. He still believed that when she left he would be sad but would get over it as he always had in the past. He knew he would miss their lovemaking.

He had never had a woman previously who

understood his wants and needs as she did. He realized he would never find someone else who would anticipate his desires like her. And he liked the feeling of satisfying her so completely. He had been searching his whole life for a relationship like they were sharing. He wondered if he could ever find another woman who would satisfy him again as she did. And he was beginning to realize he did not even want to look for anyone else.

He was not thinking realistically. He still thought the worst that would happen was he would be away from her for seven months and then she would be back in Seattle the following summer.

He even started thinking that maybe they could take a cruise together in the spring that would break up their time apart. He had already blocked from his mind how he had trouble sleeping when she was away on her trips; in addition how he could not sleep without her last night. He also did not think about how food did not taste very good and how he barely ate when she was away from him.

Feeling a lot better when she woke up she knew Chase would have been shocked and upset if he knew the direction her thoughts were taking. Realizing he would never change she knew she needed to get past the negative feelings she was having towards him. There were so few days left and she wanted to enjoy her last moments with him. She was now becoming resigned to never seeing him again.

That evening the two of them decided to eat dinner at a little restaurant in town. They had a wonderful salmon dinner they both enjoyed. However tonight, unlike Victoria, as they went back to the boat the clouds blocked the sky so there was not a sunset to view. They went to bed early and as the boat rocked with the waves their lovemaking had a passion they had not experienced before.

The next morning was a typical day after a storm. The sun was shining and the sea was totally calm. No one would guess the tumult that went on the day before. Leaving Winter Harbor right after breakfast they made Ucluelet by late in the afternoon.

As on the other days they had dinner on the boat and watched the sunset. They were going to stay an extra day but once again the weatherman was talking about an upcoming storm.

Chase thought it was best for them to head for Victoria and get away from the open sea. They reached Victoria by mid-afternoon and knew there would be enough time to head towards Orcas Island. After they fueled the boat at the marina they cancelled their berth for the night. Then they headed for their favorite destination.

This would be their last chance to anchor off the island by the cabin before their trip ended. Since they had first made love in the cabin they wanted some extra time by this island as a final farewell on their journey together.

It was the end of day eight when they dropped the anchor, knowing they would still have enough time to spend a day and a half here. They ate dinner and then held hands while watching the sunset. She had a feeling when she got back to Wisconsin it would be a long time before she could watch a sunset without feeling very sad.

They spent the next day on the boat. Neither of them was very hungry. Most of the day found them in bed. They spent hours holding each other without saying much. She kept hoping he would tell her that he loved her but he never said a word. For the present she was just satisfied to stay wrapped in his arms.

By the time they set sail back to the marina she was ready to go to Wisconsin. The thought of leaving him made her ache but she knew she could not continue to stay in Seattle when he would not commit to her.

Joe was waiting at the pier when they docked. They both gave him a hug but he felt so sad when he saw them. He knew nothing had been resolved. He realized as far as she was concerned it was over. He also felt Chase was being very stupid. He knew he would have an extremely rough time with him when Nikki went away.

Chapter Forty-Eight

After they left the boat they returned to the condo for the night. It was Friday evening and she was leaving for Wisconsin on Monday. This would be her last time at his condo. They decided to have sandwiches from the leftover boat food.

Sitting in his kitchen with a plate of food in front of her, she looked at him with anguish.

"Chase, we need to talk."

"Can't we keep this light and uncomplicated, Nikki?"

"I am leaving on Monday. Being light and uncomplicated is not going to work. I know you want to act like nothing is going to happen but it is. I am leaving and I am not planning on ever coming back here."

What she said did not really sink into him and he never noticed the tears in her eyes.

"You know I was thinking I could take some extra time off and drive with you to Wisconsin. That way you would not have to make that long trip by yourself. Then I will just fly back to Seattle. I was also wondering if we could take a cruise together next spring.

"Chase, you are not listening to me. I said I was never coming back to Seattle. I don't plan on ever seeing or talking to you again. I need to get on with my life."

This time he heard what she was saying. As he looked at her she saw pain flash across his face.

"You do not plan to ever see me again," he asked in disbelief?

"I will not see you or talk to you ever again. What part of never do you not understand?"

"I can't fathom why you would never want to see me again?" as he shook his head in disbelief at her.

"How can you not understand," she moaned? "I just cannot do this anymore. I cannot keep leaving you and then come back over and over. I guess I lied to myself when I told you I did not want any strings or commitments. Either that or I changed my mind. You are both my lover and my best friend but I know your life has no room for commitments. I told you neither of us would be clingy. We needed each other for this season and did what we had to do. But when you kiss me good-bye I need us to be over."

She could hardly look at him as she told him how she felt. She could not believe the pain she was feeling.

"I think I want to be alone tonight," she sobbed.

All he did was look at her with disbelief in his eyes. Since she still had all her things in the car she stood up from the kitchen table, leaned down and kissed him on the cheek. Then she turned quickly and ran out the door leaving all of her sandwich still sitting on the plate.

As he watched her leave he had no clue what had just happened. All he felt was a terrible ache deep inside of him as she left his house.

All the way back to the boat, tears streamed down her face. She almost pulled to the side of the road but knew she might not leave that spot all night if she started crying too hard. She needed to make it to the marina before totally breaking down.

The next day was spent in a daze packing the rest

of her belongings for her trip home. Since it was Saturday she wondered if perhaps she should not leave on Sunday instead of waiting for Monday. She tried to keep herself busy and block Chase from her mind. She could not believe she would never again sleep through the night with him or feel his arms around her.

About 5:00 p.m. there was a knock on her door. Glancing out the window she saw Chase standing there. He looked as terrible as she felt. She realized he had not gotten much sleep the night before either. He had such a sad expression on his face all she wanted to do was hold him.

Instead she opened the door and stood back as he walked in.

"I know you wanted to be alone last night but we have tonight and tomorrow to be together before you leave. And I still want to drive with you to Wisconsin. Can't we have these last few days together, Nikki?"

As she looked at him, she knew she would not be able to refuse any of his requests. She moved towards him, put her arms tightly around his neck, and kissed him hard. As she felt his body against hers, she knew she needed these last memories of him.

Knowing she was delaying the inevitable, she could not help herself. He still didn't get it! But she wanted to spend every last moment with him that was possible.

As they lay in bed he refused to say anything about their relationship. But she was now able to accept this. At least he did not talk about meeting her in some future time. That was a subject she would not allow him to bring up ever again.

When he fell asleep she knew he had not slept any more than she had the previous night. However she still could not sleep. She lay in his arms and watched him.

She wanted to memorize his face. About three hours later he woke up. When he saw her looking at him, they both forgot anything else as their lips met.

The next morning they finished packing her car to go back to his place. The condo was closer to the interstate on the south side of town, and therefore they would not encounter rush hour when leaving the next day. She also wanted to have one last dinner with Joe.

She gazed sadly around the houseboat before they closed and locked the door. She left the key at the marina office. Walking to her car she thought about the many happy memories of her time spent here at the marina. She felt very melancholy that she would never live here again. But it was time to move on.

She had said good-bye to Brooke on Saturday morning. She and Brandon were still calling and emailing each other. The two of them had planned a trip together over the holidays and Nikki knew she would see her at that time.

With tears in her eyes they met Joe for dinner. She had a terrible feeling she might never see him again. She hugged him extra hard after dinner when they were leaving. She told him to take good care of Chase. They both knew Chase could not comprehend what he would go through when he got back to Seattle and she was gone. But it was time for her to get back to her old life; a life that did not include Chase.

Chapter Forty-Nine

Leaving Seattle at 7:00 a.m. they took turns driving and traveled I-90 through the state of Washington and Idaho. They pulled into Missoula, Montana, at 6:00 p.m. They wanted to be in their hotel early so they could spend as much time as possible together in the evening. Chase was finally becoming resigned to the fact that he would never see her again.

Neither of them slept well. They kept waking up throughout the night and made love or snuggled whenever they awoke. Besides wanting to touch each other as much as possible they wanted as many last precious moments together before their final good-bye.

The next morning they left the hotel at 8:00 a.m. Their lodging had a continental breakfast so they knew they did not have to stop for breakfast. Besides, neither of them could choke down much food anyway. They also carried a pillow and blanket in the car so the person not driving could sleep.

It seemed liked the miles went by in a blur. One part of her wanted to get to Wisconsin but the other part wanted to stay on the road forever if he would be by her side. They barely got over the border into North Dakota the second night.

They stayed in a little town called Dickinson. That

evening was a repeat of the night before. They would only sleep about two hours and then would awaken. Thank goodness they could sleep in the car she thought.

The third day they made it to St. Cloud, Minnesota. She knew it would take them about seven hours the next day to reach Milwaukee. The closer they got to Wisconsin the sadder they both became.

They planned to stay at a hotel in Milwaukee out at the airport. She did not want him to come to her house. Despite her husband's coma state she was still legally married and it did not seem right to make love to Chase in the home she and Ted had shared.

They arrived at their Milwaukee hotel about 4:00 p.m. They were staying at a suite hotel so they stopped to buy some food. They did not need a lot since neither of them was very hungry but they also did not want to waste time going out to eat. They just wanted to spend their last moments alone.

They were up all night. The two of them were sleep deprived but they knew their time together was ticking away and they did not want to spend their last hours sleeping. She remembered the first time she had ever slept on the plane. It was July a year and a half ago and she was on a journey; a journey where she would meet Chase for the first time. Now they would be leaving each other forever and he could sleep on the plane back to Seattle.

They finally fell asleep about 5:00 a.m. They awoke at 8:00 a.m. Checkout time was noon and his plane was at 1:45 p.m. They got out of bed at 11:30 a.m. and took one last shower together. At exactly noon she pulled out of the hotel parking lot and headed for the airport. She pulled up to the departure door.

She got out of the car and gave him a hug. Their lips met for one last kiss. She kept her composure as steely as possible. She had promised herself she would not cry or break down in front of him. While they were kissing, an airport guard came up to them and broke them apart.

"You have to move that car right now or you are going to get a ticket."

This time he moved away from her, turned rapidly and walked quickly into the terminal with his duffel bag in hand. He never looked back and he made it to the gate before the tears began streaming down his cheeks.

It was just after 1:00 p.m. when she parked in the garage and entered her condo. She knew Chase would be boarding his plane in a few minutes. She could not believe what she had been through in the last five months. Even without Chase in her life she knew she would miss Seattle. She sensed she belonged there now. It felt like home to her. She shook her head. That part of her life was over. She had to let go of Seattle and more importantly, Chase.

She noticed all her boxes had arrived and her sons had brought them into the living room for her. All of her belongings she had brought from Seattle were still in her vehicle. She went out to the car and got the pillow that she and Chase had shared. When she laid down on her bed she could smell him. She put her face into the pillow and began sobbing uncontrollably.

The next morning she could barely function. She carried all the things in from her car and called her sons to let them know she was home safely. She made a date to meet them for dinner in a few days. She also called Joe and let him know she was home. When he asked her how she was she began crying so hard she had to break the connection. It would be a week before she could call him again.

Chapter Fifty

Nikki sat staring at all of her boxes that weekend but was unable to do anything except sit in her chair and cry. She wanted to pick up the phone and call Chase. If only she could hear his voice one more time. However she realized if she called him, she would lose all her resolve and be back on a plane to Seattle as soon as she could make the reservation. She knew she had to take control of her life again but figured it would not hurt to sit and feel sorry for herself for a couple of days.

Kyle found her sitting in her living room chair Monday after work. He could not believe the way his mother looked. Her eyes were red from crying and her face looked sunken in. He realized right away she had not been eating anything. She looked at Kyle and said she would start on her boxes soon. She told him she was letting Chase go.

Her son had no idea his mother's feelings towards her friend ran so deep. Kyle had a friend; a psychiatrist named Matt. He called his friend immediately. Within thirty minutes the doctor arrived.

Matt asked Kyle to go into the kitchen while he talked to his mother. He told her he would give her some medicine for her depression however she refused to take any. As she continued to talk to the doctor he realized she had a grasp of reality. She just needed to get over the shock of losing a man she loved so deeply.

Matt then asked her if she had been sleeping and she told him no. She had been too busy focusing on all the wonderful memories she and Chase had shared the last few months to sleep. The doctor told her he would not give her the medicine for depression unless she could not get out of her funk. However he was going to insist she take a sedative to help her sleep since she was so sleep deprived. He knew if she got some sleep she would probably start feeling a little better.

Kyle was so worried about his mother he immediately called Brandon. By the time Matt had gotten Nikki to sleep Brandon came in the door. The psychologist told both boys he thought their mother would be all right but they needed to watch her for the next few days.

The doctor felt if she began getting back to a normal routine she would probably be able to conquer her depression. Matt did tell the boys that her mental health was in a very precarious state. Some people never got over losing someone they loved that much.

Sleeping a little over twenty-four hours she awoke the next evening and found both Kyle and Brandon there. She could not believe she had lost all of Tuesday. She also realized she felt better.

The boys tried to ask her some questions about her relationship with Chase but she told them it was over and she never wanted to hear his name spoken again. Her two sons were afraid she might go over the edge if they pressed her and all they wanted was for their mother to be well again.

Although she still ached for Chase she did not feel like crying constantly. The boys fixed her some soup and insisted she eat a little so she would not get sick. Matt had left an extra sleeping pill for her. He wanted her to get one more good night's rest and her two sons made sure she took it. They both stayed with her until she fell back to sleep.

When she awoke Wednesday morning she knew she was going to be okay. She actually felt like unpacking a few boxes. She worked on putting her belongings away for the next two days and the boys insisted she go out to dinner with them both nights. Little by little she felt she was returning to the land of the living.

On Friday she met with Ted's doctor. His health was still deteriorating. Some of his body functions were starting to shut down. The doctor did not think he would last until Christmas.

This made her sad. She had been with Ted for many years. However she also felt better, too. She was thinking of selling her home to help with the medical bills. But more importantly she knew Ted would hate to be alive as he was in his vegetative state.

Preparing her sons for their father's death would also be hard. Even though Ted had really left them on the operating table the boys still thought of him as alive. It would be a shock when their father actually died and had to be buried.

She was finally ready to call Joe back. She missed talking to him and had not heard from him since the day she had hung up on him in tears. She decided to wait until Sunday night because she knew how busy the restaurant was on the weekends.

Joe was delighted to hear from her when she finally called him. He knew she had her family to help her over the loss of Chase but he had still been worried about what she would go through. She told him how she was once again taking control of her life which made him happy. She also confessed to him about her sons calling the doctor and how she had slept for almost two days. Finally she told him about the doctor's prognosis for Ted.

She was afraid to ask Joe about Chase. However he sensed she wanted to know about him. Without her asking he told her that Chase was not doing very well. Like her, Chase had sat in his living room chair for three days and had not moved to clean up or to eat. He did not think his friend had slept any more than she had during that time.

After he tried to get him up and moving without success Joe had gone back to the restaurant and gotten his bartender Kevin. The man weighed three hundred pounds and was over six feet. Together the two of them had forced Chase out of his chair and made him shave and shower. They also insisted he eat some soup they had brought along. That action brought Chase back to reality. She winced when she heard what Joe was saying about Chase.

Joe told her Chase was doing a little better now. He had gone back to work and he came into the restaurant every night for dinner. She knew she did not need to worry about Chase. Joe would take good care of him until he could come to grips with the reality of her leaving.

He did not tell her that Chase never smiled anymore or that he had lost fifteen pounds in the two weeks since he had left her. He knew she would lose her resolve and come back. He was smart enough to know Chase had to make the first move.

"Would you ever come back to him, Nikki?"

"I would be out there as soon as a plane could get me there and stay forever if he told me he loved me."

"I thought that was how you felt. I know it is really hard but you are doing the right thing."

"I do feel better but sometimes I feel so much pain at the thought of him never holding me again in his arms."

"That pain will never go away but it will lessen with

time. Trust me on that."

She knew he was thinking of his beloved wife when he was talking to her about the pain lessening.

After the conversation ended she felt a lot better and was ready to get on with her life. The week after Thanksgiving she flew to San Antonio, Texas for a six-day tour. This would be her last trip of the year. She had just arrived back at the Milwaukee airport at the end of that tour when her cell phone rang.

The long-term care facility was calling. Ted was dying. They had contacted her two sons and they thought she should come directly to be with her husband. She met her sons at the facility and they went in to see him. As they stood there Ted let go. She knew she should feel bad but instead she felt relief. She hoped he had not suffered while he was in his coma state.

They buried him two days later. She had left Ted emotionally months before but now she knew another chapter in her life had closed. She was not sure where her next journey would take her but she looked forward to the future with anticipation.

Christmas would not be a very happy occasion. It had only been a year ago when the whole family had spent Christmas in New Orleans. This year Nikki's brother Randy would be with them again. Brooke was also coming.

She told everyone she thought they should go on a cruise to welcome in the New Year. So many sad things had happened to her this last year but she also had more moments of happiness than some people ever found in a lifetime.

Nikki made arrangements for their cruise. Brooke was going to stay in her cabin and the boys would have a separate room. She then called Joe. She told him Randy needed a cabin mate. She wanted to see him again and thought a New Year's cruise would be perfect since he could still spend Christmas in Seattle. She was so excited when Joe said "yes."

Chapter Fifty-One

Christmas was very bittersweet that year as she knew it would be. The boys missed their father but they knew even if he had still been alive he would not have been with them physically. It also helped that they spent the holiday at home since it did not remind them of being away the previous year. And Brooke was spending the holidays with them and it was hard not to feel happiness with her and Brandon's developing relationship.

Nikki was feeling closer to her each time they were together and was hoping she might become her daughter-in-law. Brooke had talked to her about Chase one afternoon when they were alone together. Although she did not want to speak about him to her sons for some reason she felt better telling Brooke how she felt about him. She wondered if the two of them did not have empathy for each other over the pain of losing someone they had loved so much. Like Joe, Brooke also reiterated that the pain would never go away but would lessen with time.

She still could not stop thinking about Chase. There were nights when she woke up in the middle of the night dreaming she was in his arms again. The dreams were so vivid that she often would cry for a few minutes. The pain had finally lessened but there was a constant dull ache. She wondered if she would ever get over the hurt.

She had gone to talk to Matt for a couple of sessions. He told her she was on the right track and doing fine. He knew she was a strong person. Many people might not have weathered what she had. She had lost weight but even the doctor had told her it was becoming on her.

Matt realized how deep her love for Chase was. He could not help but wonder how her lover was fairing. The doctor knew if Chase loved Nikki as deeply as she loved him then he had to be in deep trouble. He knew it would take him some time before he got over the denial phase since he had never addressed that issue as Nikki had. Acceptance was not going to come easy to the man Matt suspected.

Two days after Christmas they all flew down to Florida for their seven-day Eastern Caribbean cruise. She thought briefly of how Ted would have stayed in his cabin watching movies or just followed her around. Instead she felt great joy at what a fun time the family would have being together.

As they exited the plane and walked into the gate area, Joe was waiting for them. His plane had come in a half and hour before their plane. She ran to him and hugged him tight.

"It is so good to see you again. I really missed you."

As she looked at him she knew he had not changed since she had last seen him, but there was something different in his eyes.

She could tell Joe was pleased to see her and blushed when she hugged him. He knew looking at her that if she and Chase never got back together again she would be okay. But he was also a little sad because he realized there would never be anyone else in her life. He did not want her to have to live an empty life forever like he had been doing since Theresa's death.

He understood more clearly than ever that the

two of them were meant to be together again. He was still eating dinner with his friend every night. Although he was doing better, not only had he lost almost twenty-five pounds, he had also lost the glimmer he used to have in his eyes.

Joe had a plan to get them back together but he knew Chase had to first understand how much he loved Nikki. She was his destiny but for some reason he was too stubborn to realize it. Every night he would tell Joe how well he was doing without her. Many times Joe felt like asking him if he ever really looked in a mirror since she had left.

Before Joe left for the cruise he asked his friend at dinner one night, "Why do you want to live like this? You are alone and you had a woman who loved you with all her heart. Why would you throw that away? Do you have any idea how many people never find a love like you two had? I am going on my cruise over New Year's but I want you to think about what I have just said. You are a fool, Chase, if you think you are happy without her."

With that Joe shook his head at him and got off the barstool. Chase watched him walk away with still no understanding.

The six of them had a lot of fun on their cruise. They went snorkeling and spent a lot of time at the ports of call. This time she did not sit at a little café alone having her afternoon beer. Joe and sometimes the others would join her.

New Year's Eve they were on the outside deck when the midnight hour arrived. There was something wonderful being on the deck of a ship on New Year's Eve. As the streamers went sailing through the air she looked up at the full moon and all the stars twinkling in the sky. What a perfect moment! Only one thing was missing. Everyone kissed and hugged and she was so happy she was able to be with her sons and brother and her new friend Joe.

She would have been very unhappy to know Chase was sitting at home alone. He was thinking of what Joe had said to him that night at dinner before he left for the cruise. As midnight approached he suddenly realized his friend was right. He was a fool! He missed everything about Nikki but especially sleeping with her in his arms.

He had a terrible ache in his heart that began the moment he walked away from her at the Milwaukee airport. He did not know if he could do anything about the situation but at least he had finally reached the acceptance stage.

He whispered out loud, "I love you, Nikki, with my whole heart and soul." There was no one to hear him but he slept soundly through the night for the first time since the two of them had parted.

New Year's Day there was happy family news. Brooke and Brandon were engaged! Everyone was happy but Nikki realized that meant he would move to Seattle the following summer.

Before they knew it the cruise was over. As Joe left them at the airport she hugged him once again very hard.

"I am really going to miss you. Why don't we do this again next year?"

Joe told her that sounded like fun but he knew next year he would not be around anymore. He wanted to be with Theresa more than ever. It was almost time for him to go. He did not want her to know what he was thinking. He was hoping that next year she would be cruising with Chase.

She decided to put her home up for sale. It was too big with the boys and Ted gone. She decided she needed to downsize her life. She was not sure if she would buy a small condo or just rent an apartment. There was time to deal with that later. Both of her sons thought she was making a wise decision and were happy she was handling all the change in her life so well.

Chapter Fifty-Two

Joe could not believe his eyes when he got back to Seattle. Chase had picked him up in the same lot he used to pick up Nikki. He saw instantly there was something different in his friend's demeanor. He finally understood how deep his love for Nikki was.

As Joe looked at him, Chase said, "Yes, I love her with my whole heart and soul but I don't know what to do about it. She has gone on with her life and I am not sure how to get her back."

"I will help you, Chase, if you want me to. I think this is the reason why I am still living—to help you two get back together."

"I would be eternally grateful for any help from you."

Joe was busy over the next few weeks although they continued to eat dinner together every night. Chase was beginning to gain back a little of his lost weight. He still did not have the twinkle in his eyes but he smiled from time to time.

One evening Joe asked him to go out with him on the boat the following Saturday. They spent the day in the Sound going from island to island and stopping for lunch by Orcas Island. Joe seemed happier than Chase had seen him in a long time.

Monday night was Valentine's Day. Chase thought about Nikki all day. He wanted to talk to Joe about her but when he came in for dinner he was not there. He was worried about his friend especially since Joe had made a comment about seeing him tonight. Knowing how busy the restaurant was on this particular evening he had a terrible feeling about his friend.

Chase asked Kevin to go with him to Joe's house. Kevin had a key from the restaurant. As they entered his home the first thing they saw placed on the table by the entryway was a huge vase filled with red roses. Chase looked at the card. It said, "Happy Valentine's Day, my darling Theresa!"

They found Joe in his bedroom. He was lying down on the bed with a rose in his hand and there was a smile on his face. He immediately felt a stab of pain that his friend and father figure was gone. But now knowing what he felt for Nikki, he knew Joe was finally where he needed to be—with his darling Theresa.

Realizing Nikki needed to be informed, he did not feel comfortable calling her himself. Joe had taken care of all his final arrangements but he wanted to help Joe's lawyer with the details.

He asked the lawyer to call Nikki. He knew she would want to come to the funeral. They set the service for Thursday so that would give her time to fly there. The lawyer told him that he needed to meet with both of them the day after the funeral.

When the lawyer called she cried when she heard about Joe. She immediately called for an airline ticket for her trip to Seattle for the funeral. She left the return open.

She did not want to stay any longer than necessary however the lawyer had told her he needed to discuss some things with her on Friday. Since she was not sure how long the meeting would last it was just easier to have an open return ticket. The lawyer had also arranged a hotel room for her.

As much as she did not want to see Chase and hated the reason she was here it felt good to be back in Seattle. She had missed the city. It was Wednesday 2:00 p.m. Pacific Time when her plane touched down.

The lawyer said someone would meet her at baggage to take her to the wake and then to her hotel. When she arrived at baggage she did not see anyone holding her name up on a sign. She decided when she got her luggage she would take the Super Shuttle to the funeral parlor since she had the address.

As she reached for her suitcase an arm reached over hers and grabbed the bag off the carousel. As she looked up she saw Chase.

Turning white when she saw him, she hoped he did not notice. She knew she would be seeing him sometime during the services but she had not been prepared to see him at the airport.

Chase noted her reaction to him but decided to ignore it. Instead he casually said, "Hi, Nikki."

"I did not know you would be coming to pick me up. I could have walked to the holding area."

"Would you have walked out there to meet me?"

"Probably not."

She noticed he winced when she said that.

After they got to his car they drove most of the way to the funeral parlor in silence. It was a very uncomfortable silence but he did not really care. He was with her again and it felt good just having her so close. Finally she asked him to tell her about Joe's death.

He told her about finding Joe in bed with the smile on his face and about the vase of red roses for his late wife.

"I am going to miss him so much. I am so sad to lose him but I am also glad he is with Theresa again."

"I feel exactly the same way."

Asking about her sons she told him about Brandon and Brooke getting engaged.

"Will they live here in Seattle?"

"I guess."

At that point she turned her head to look out the car window. She was having a hard time pretending to have an ordinary conversation with him. He realized how difficult it was for her to be in such a small enclosure with him. He decided not to say anything else; just being near her made his heart soar.

When they arrived at the funeral parlor she immediately went up to the front of the room and stood by Joe's coffin. She looked at him for a long time. She could feel Chase walk up beside her.

She did not know how she was going to make it through the next couple of days with him always next to her. Since she was not looking at him, she could not see the hunger in his eyes as he looked down at her.

It was extremely uncomfortable for her with him constantly next to her. It was taking all her strength to keep her composure around him. She desperately wanted him to move away from her and was about to say something when she glanced at Joe.

For some reason she could not fathom she felt Joe would be upset if she told Chase to move away from her. She decided she could just grin and bear it for the next two days. Before she knew it she would be back in Milwaukee and would never have to see him again.

The funeral ended up not being as sad as she had anticipated. Everyone knew how Joe had felt about Theresa and the whole affair turned into a celebration of his life.

Chase barely spoke to her but he also never left her side whenever they were together. He made sure he was the one to drive her to her hotel both nights. He never said a word to her while they were driving and just dropped her off at the front door. Just being in the same space as her was all he needed for the present.

She was glad he was acting cool towards her. If he had tried to talk to her she probably would have started crying and she did not want to show any emotion around him. Worse yet she knew if he had asked to go up to her room she would not have been able to refuse him. She wanted to touch him so badly she ached, and was extremely upset the sight of him could still do that to her.

He told her he would pick her up Friday morning at 9:30 a.m. to go to the lawyer's office. She just nodded her head at him. As she got out of the car he handed her an envelope.

Entering her room all she could think about was a long soak in a hot bath. She put the note from Chase on her bedside table. She then spent the next forty-five minutes soaking in the bathtub. She was so emotionally drained from Joe's funeral and being so close to Chase again she could not stop the tears from running down her cheeks. She could hardly wait to get back to Milwaukee and as far away from him as possible.

As she got out of the bathtub her telephone rang. Brandon and Kyle were calling to see how the funeral went and how she was doing. They did not mention Chase but she knew they were worried about her.

She told them everything went well and she was fine. She did not want them to know how hard the situation had been for her and tried to keep her answers light. She then told the boys she was not sure how long she would be tied up the next day at the attorney's office but she thought she would probably fly back early Saturday morning.

She planned to call for her return flight as soon as she finished with the lawyer. As long as she as was back in Seattle she thought she would spend some time downtown the next afternoon and evening. She told her sons she would call them and let them know her flight schedule as soon as she made the reservation.

As she hung up the phone she glanced down and saw Chase's note. Her first reaction was to throw it away without reading it. Then she decided if he went to the trouble of writing her a note the least she could do was read it.

Opening the envelope she started reading. "Nikki," the note started. "I know you will be going back to Milwaukee this weekend. It pains me when I realize how much I have hurt you. I assumed you would not want to talk to me tomorrow when we go to the lawyer's office so I wanted to write you this note. Even if I never see you again I want you to know I love you with my whole heart and soul. I now know how painful it was for Joe to live without Theresa after she died. I want to spend the rest of my life with you. I don't know if you can forgive me for not acknowledging my love for you. Please grow old with me. Love, Chase."

She could not stop the tears after reading his note. She knew how much pain he had to go through to reach this point. And she had noticed he had lost weight but had never said anything to him. She had been afraid to say anything to him for fear of breaking down.

It was almost an hour later after reading his note that she was knocking on his door.

As he opened the door she heard him say, "I did not think you would come, Nikki."

She threw her arms around his neck as their lips

met eagerly. She could not believe he had admitted that he loved her as much as she loved him.

They were awake all night talking and making love. They decided they would have to take a nap when they got back from the lawyer's office. She could not help but wonder how lucky they had been to come together again. It had taken Joe's death to help them find their way back to each other. She felt sad about that but knew Joe was happy where he now was.

Before they knew it morning was upon them and they drove to the attorney's office. When they arrived at the lawyer's office, his secretary took them right in.

The lawyer told them they were both in Joe's will. Although it would take several months for probate Joe had transferred some of his property into their names. The two of them looked at each other in surprise. They really had not expected anything from Joe. They were so thankful he had come into their lives. They knew it was because of him that they were back together again.

Joe had left the boat to both of them. There was a stipulation that they could not sell the boat unless they married someone else, until one of them died. Their friend wanted to make sure they would find a way back to each other.

The lawyer said they could consider the boat theirs immediately. Chase looked at her with a twinkle in his eyes. Smiling back at him as she read his mind she knew instantly where they would be spending their afternoon naptime.

The lawyer said Joe had a distant nephew he had left the restaurant to. He was not sure if the nephew would keep the restaurant or sell it. He had also made some small bequests to some of his employees.

The last item shocked them. Joe had always been

interested in Chase's work. He had invested in a small motorcoach company with three buses several years ago. The business was doing well. His partner wanted to retire and just before Joe had died he had bought his partner out. The company now belonged to both of them jointly. Obviously he wanted to make sure they were tied together.

Neither of them could believe that Joe had made their dreams come true. They left the law office with tears in their eyes. As they drove to their boat, "Journey Ahead," Nikki called her sons to tell them all the news

When they got to the marina all thoughts of a nap left them as they walked to the boat and went below. Later they would talk about all the wonderful things that had happened to them today. At the moment all they could think about was being together again.

If anyone could have looked inside the boat they would have seen a trail of clothes strewn all over the floor from the main cabin into their bedroom. Nikki and Chase were home and together forever.

About the Author

Kileen Prather was born in 1947 in Superior, Wis., and graduated from the University of Wisconsin-Madison with a B.A. in History and a M.A. in School Librarianship from Central Michigan University. Before becoming a writer, she was a school librarian for 21 years and has been a tour manager since 1998. She usually travels in at least 35 states a year and meets wonderful travelers from all over the country who have given her inspiration for her stories. She presently divides her time between Texas and Wisconsin. She is a mother of two boys, Frank & Rick, and grandmother of Isabel.

People who have experienced life over the years are the focus for her books in these modern day romance stories. Their hearts and souls are constantly developing and growing due to the simple fact that they have "lived." The mature reader can relate to the characters' hopes and dreams because of their age, relationships, and experiences. Younger readers can learn what it is like to face life while dealing with its challenges or possibly relate it to someone in their lives.

Her stories take place in various locales in the United States since mature adults have experienced travel, like to travel, or at least dream about going to different places. These characters are ordinary people struggling with issues aging adults have to face such as changing spousal relationships, parental concerns, or illnesses. Many women and men find themselves divorced or widowed after 25, 35, or even 45 years of marriage. These devastating experiences seem to halt life as they know it. They often don't believe it is possible to start over or lead a fulfilling life. They need to know that "living" takes place and "romance is possible" no matter what your age.

Other Books by Kileen Prather

Journey Beckons
Journey to Port
Journey to the Tropics